Lions

EMERGENCY

Panic set in. The two girls screamed as they were kicked by other dancers. A scuffle broke out. The bouncers fought their way across the floor. Everybody was yelling. There was complete confusion. Nobody could see what was happening. The music thumped on relentlessly and the dancing continued.

Bella was terrified. She began beating people away with her fists.

'Stay back!' she pleaded. 'He's ill. Can't you see - stay back!'

Other titles in the City Hospital series

New Blood
Flames
Fever

EMERGENCY

KEITH MILES

Lions

An imprint of HarperCollins*Publishers*

First published in Great Britain in Lions 1995
Lions is an imprint of HarperCollins Publishers Ltd
77-85 Fulham Palace Road, Hammersmith
London W6 8JB

1 3 5 7 9 8 6 4 2

Copyright © Keith Miles 1995

The author asserts the moral right to be identified
as the author of this work.

ISBN 0 00 675090 7

Set in Stempel Garamond

Printed and bound in Great Britain by
HarperCollins Manufacturing, Glasgow

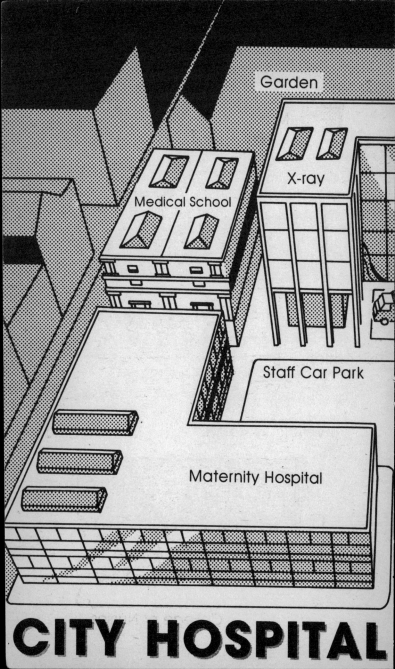

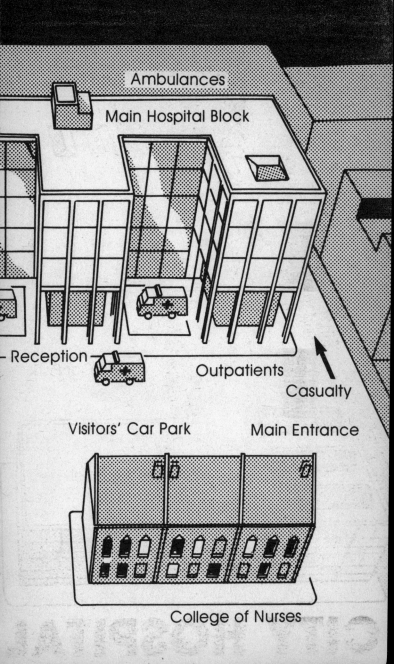

Ambulances

Main Hospital Block

Reception

Outpatients

Casualty

Visitors' Car Park

Main Entrance

College of Nurses

Gordy sensed trouble at once. As he and Bella were going into the disco, a guy was being thrown out by two of the bouncers. There was a strong sense of menace about the place. It was dark and claustrophobic. Behind the pounding of the music was an air of pent-up violence waiting to explode.

Gordy Robbins looked around with misgiving. He had to shout to make himself heard above the pulsing noise.

'Maybe this isn't such a good idea, Bel.'

'Why not?'

'It just doesn't feel right.'

She laughed. 'That's the attraction.'

'Is it always this rough?' he shouted.

'Yes, Gordy. That's why I like it here.'

They'd both worked late at the hospital and felt the need to relax and unwind. When Bella suggested an hour at a new club, Gordy was happy to go along. He was having second thoughts now. *Underworld* seemed to be full of heavy guys in leather jackets. Even the girls looked at him aggressively.

Bella Denton, on the other hand, seemed completely at home.

'Isn't this music fab?' she said. She was already moving in time to the sounds.

'I need a drink,' said Gordy.

'C'mon Gordy, let's dance first.' She pulled him towards the dancers.

Before they could join the floor, they were accosted by a tall, slim boy in jeans. His long hair was tied back in a ponytail and he had stubble on his chin. Arms outspread, he welcomed Bella like an old friend.

'Hi! Great to see you again.'

'Oh... yes,' she said, half-recognising him. 'Hello.'

'We met here last week,' he reminded her. 'Don't say you've forgotten me? Adam. My name's Adam.'

'Hi, Adam.'

'And you are... wait a minute... yeah - Bella!'

'That's right,' she said. 'This is Gordy.'

Adam nodded in Gordy's direction but he was only interested in Bella. His eyes glittered with excitement. Bella vaguely remembered having met him with a gang of others on her last visit. She liked his easy smile and his cool manner.

'OK then, babe. Dance?'

Bella grinned. 'Why not?'

He took her hand and led her away.

'What about me?' complained Gordy.

'See you later,' she said, blowing him a kiss.

Gordy was miffed. He'd only gone to *Underworld* at her suggestion. Within a minute of being there, Bella had dumped him for someone whose name she couldn't even remember. Gordy made his way to the bar and bought himself a beer.

He could just pick out Adam and Bella in the strobe lighting. They were dancing energetically. As Gordy watched, a rangy figure approached them. There was a brief argument then Adam pushed the newcomer away and he retreated to the edge of the dance floor. Gordy couldn't make out what was happening.

Bella was annoyed. 'Who was that?' she asked.

'Some creep,' said Adam. 'Forget him.'

'But what did he want?' she insisted. 'Why did he threaten you like that?'

'Let's dance.' Adam ignored her question.

He moved smoothly to the rhythm of the music and Bella responded. They were soon caught up in it. He was a good dancer and she was enjoying herself. After a long day at the hospital, she was in a mood for fun. Bella didn't even notice when Adam's movements became more and more frenzied.

Waving his arms wildly and twisting his hips, Adam was starting to bump into other people. They protested loudly and shoved him back but he ignored them. Adam was in a world of his own; his eyes were glazed, his teeth fixed in a manic grin.

The music was deafening and Adam was dancing frantically now, flailing around and yelling with excitement. He was hitting people indiscriminately. Then, without warning, he seemed to lose control.

His head fell forward, his body sagged and his legs turned to jelly. He collapsed so heavily against Bella that he knocked her backwards into another couple. All four of them fell to the floor with a sickening thud.

Panic set in. The two girls screamed as they were kicked by other dancers. A scuffle broke out. The bouncers fought their way across the floor. Everybody was yelling. There was complete confusion. Nobody could see what was happening. The music thumped on relentlessly and the dancing continued.

Bella was terrified. She began beating people away with her fists.

'Stay back!' she pleaded. 'He's ill. Can't you see — stay back!'

The other couple had got straight up again but Adam was still motionless, lying on his back in the middle of the floor. Bella feared the worst. The dancers were all around them again, threatening to trample on Adam at any moment.

'Keep away!' she screamed. 'He'll get hurt!'

The scuffle had become a free-for-all and the bouncers were having difficulty quelling it. It was pandemonium. Gordy could see very little through the haze of cigarette smoke and dancing bodies but he knew Bella was at the centre of it all. Putting his drink down, he dived into the crowded dance floor and tried to elbow his way towards her.

'Help me someone!' she cried. 'Please help me!'

Her screams rose above the music and chaos.

'Someone's just collapsed! Give him some air!'

Gordy struggled through and eventually got to her.

'What happened, Bel?' he gasped.

'Adam - he just fell. They'll tread on him if we can't get him out of here.'

'Get back!' he shouted. 'Keep back!'

The music seemed overwhelming and the fight became more violent - the noise was deafening. Gordy and Bella tried to protect Adam's inert body. It was frightening. They were pushed and shoved and someone punched Gordy. Then, quite suddenly, there was silence — the music was turned off, the lights turned on and everyone calmed down.

Gordy took one look at the collapsed figure on the floor and shouted:

'Call an ambulance!'

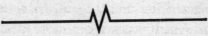

When the ambulance arrived, Gordy and Bella were still kneeling beside Adam. They turned him on his side so that he wouldn't inhale his vomit if he was sick. Gordy checked his pulse then sniffed his breath. He could detect the smell of alcohol.

Bella was shaking. She'd actually been dancing with him when he'd collapsed, she thought. It made her feel guilty for some reason. When she'd

13

managed to calm herself, her training as a student nurse won through. She made Adam as comfortable as possible and asked if the windows could be opened to let in some fresh air.

'I'll go in the ambulance with him,' she volunteered.

'But you hardly know him,' said Gordy.

'It doesn't matter. I want to go.'

'Let someone else go, Bella,' pleaded Gordy.

'There isn't anyone else,' she almost shouted at him.

Two paramedics came in with a stretcher. A mocking cheer went up from some people leaning against the bar. The paramedics examined Adam and tried to bring him round, without any success. They lifted him gently on to the stretcher as Bella gave them a full account of what had happened.

Then Adam was carried out to the waiting ambulance. As they left with the paramedics, Gordy and Bella heard the music again. *Underworld* was back in business. It was just one more incident in the life of the disco.

'I'll follow on foot,' said Gordy.

'Right,' said Bella. 'I'll meet you in Casualty.'

She got into the rear of the ambulance. As it set off, Bella glanced around the interior. She saw the first aid kit, the IPPV respirator set, the analgesic equipment, the suction equipment, the intubation kit and all the other standard features of an ambulance. She thought she'd put the hospital behind her for one night, yet here she was hurtling back towards it. One of the paramedics gave Adam a more careful examination, checking his pulse, blood pressure and breathing. He lifted his eyelids but Adam remained deeply unconscious.

'What's wrong with him?' asked Bella.

'I'm not sure yet,' he said.

'It wasn't alcohol. I've seen people drunk before and it wasn't like that at all. Adam was all pumped up; he was dancing really wildy — in a frenzy.'

The paramedic looked carefully through the young man's pockets.

'Did he take anything before this happened?' he asked.

'I was only with him for a couple of minutes,' said Bella.

'But did you see him sniffing anything - solvents, or taking any pills?'

'We only met once before - that's all.'

'So he's not really a friend of yours?'

'No,' said Bella. 'But I feel sorry for him. It really frightened me when he collapsed like that. I want to know what's wrong with him.'

'It looks as though your answer's here.'

From Adam's trouser pocket, the paramedic took out an envelope. From it he tipped three small, white pills into the palm of his hand. Bella could see tiny birds stamped into the pills.

'What are they?' she asked.

'White doves,' he said. 'A common type of Ecstasy.'

He looked down sadly at Adam's still figure on the stretcher.

'He's on drugs, love.'

Casualty was as busy as ever. The majority of seats in the waiting room were taken by people needing treatment for minor injuries. A few of them were from *Underworld*, they'd been caught up in the fight and had made their way to the nearby hospital. They sat there dejectedly, holding blood-stained pads to their split lips and cuts on their foreheads.

Casualty had been alerted by the ambulance driver to expect an urgent case. Adam was given priority; he was rushed straight through to an examination room where a doctor and his team were waiting. It was left to Bella to give what little information she could to the receptionist.

'His name?' asked the woman.

'Adam,' replied Bella.

'Surname?'

'I don't know.'

'Address?'

'No idea, I'm afraid. I only met him twice.'

'Twice too often,' murmured Gordy, at her shoulder.

The receptionist looked up. She was a plump, middle-aged woman with horn-rimmed spectacles. Even under the pressure of night-duty, she managed to stay polite and cheerful.

'Is there anything you can tell me about him?'

she asked with a wry smile.

'There's nothing we can do here, Bel,' said Gordy. 'They'll look after him now. We might as well get home.'

'I can't leave the guy on his own.'

'Why not tell me what happened?' said the woman, pen poised in her hand. 'Where were you?'

'*Underworld*,' said Bella. 'The new disco in Wilson Road.'

The receptionist sighed. 'Oh, yes. We know all about *Underworld*. In the six weeks it's been open, we've had a steady stream people from there.' She sounded a warning note. 'Take my advice and stay away from that disco. There's an active drug scene there, by all accounts. And a lot of violence. Don't get mixed up in it.'

'We won't,' said Bella. 'We only dropped in to have a look at the place. Then we met Adam.'

'He met us, you mean,' said Gordy. 'He spotted Bel and dragged her off to the dance floor straightaway.'

'What sort of a state was he in?' asked the woman.

Bella told her everything that had happened, trying to piece together in her own mind the symptoms Adam had shown. The receptionist wrote down the important details on her form. It was a slow process. Gordy hovered impatiently.

When it was all over, they were asked to wait.

They found a couple of seats in a corner. As they sat down, Gordy remembered something.

'Who was that other guy?' he asked.

'What other guy?' said Bella.

'When you and Adam were dancing; I thought I saw someone come over to you.'

'You did. His name was Jez. I don't know what he wanted but he threatened to punch Adam. It was all over in a flash.'

'You do meet some weird blokes, Bel.'

She protested. 'I just had one dance with Adam, that's all. And that was soon over.'

'I wish we'd never gone near *Underworld*!'

They continued arguing for a few minutes until a staff nurse came for them. They were led into a small office, where the doctor in charge of Adam's case soon joined them. He was a balding man in his thirties with a long, sombre face.

'Hello,' he said. 'I'm Doctor Minton.'

They introduced themselves and the doctor looked at them both seriously before he spoke.

'You came in the ambulance with Adam Green, I hear.'

'Is that his name?' said Gordy. 'Adam Green?'

'Aren't you friends of his?'

'Well... not exactly,' said Bella. 'I bumped into him once before at the club but that was all. He was just a casual acquaintance.'

'I see.'

'How is he, Doctor Minton?' she asked.

'In a pretty bad way.'

'The paramedic in the ambulance mentioned drugs.'

'Yes,' said the doctor. 'He seems to have been taking a mix. Amphetamines, Ecstasy and heaven knows what else. Then he washed them down with alcohol. That can be a lethal cocktail.'

'Is Adam in any real danger?'

'Not this time. But it was a close call. We had to pump out his stomach. We're going to have to keep him in hospital for observation.'

Doctor Minton scrutinised their faces again.

'I have to ask you this for your own sake. Did either of you take any illegal substances at the disco?'

'Of course not!' said Bella, hotly.

'*Underworld* has already got a reputation for drugs.'

'Well, we've had nothing to do with it,' affirmed Gordy. 'We've got more sense. Bella's a student nurse here and I'm at the med. school. We know what harm drugs can do.'

The doctor's serious gaze stayed on Bella.

'You wouldn't be the first students to get involved in drugs,' he said, ruefully. 'I've seen some dreadful cases. Promising careers thrown away; young lives endangered. Adam Green is going down the same, one-way street.'

'How did you find out his name?' said Bella.

'From his motorbike licence. He still lives at home. The Clinical Nursing Manager tracked down the phone number. He spoke to Adam's father. Both parents are on their way to the hospital right now.'

'That lets us off the hook then,' said Gordy with relief. 'Come on, Bel. We can go.'

'I want to stay until his parents arrive,' she insisted. 'I sort of feel involved. I'd like to meet them and try to explain.'

'Don't get caught up in it, Bel,' said Gordy.

'The least I can do is speak to them.' She turned back to the doctor. 'What will happen to him, Doctor Minton?'

'That depends on how well he responds to treatment.'

'How long will he be kept in?'

'I don't know,' he said. 'But it could be some time.'

———⋀———

'Where on earth are they?' said Suzie before finishing her hot chocolate. 'It's nearly midnight.'

'You know Bella,' said Karlene. 'She's a night owl. Likes to burn the candle at both ends.'

'Well, I don't. Especially when I've got a long day ahead of me tomorrow.' Suppressing a yawn, she glanced across at the sofa. 'What about you, Mark?'

'Yeah,' he said, pushing his glasses up the bridge

of his nose. 'I've got a busy day ahead of me as well.'

'It's a very special day,' said Karlene, nudging Suzie with an elbow. 'Isn't it, Mark?'

He almost blushed. 'I don't know about that.'

The three friends were in the living-room of the house they shared with Bella and Gordy. Mark Andrews was another student nurse, Suzie Hembrow was training to be a radiographer and Karlene Smith was taking a three-year course to become a chartered physiotherapist.

Mark was rather shy and reticent.

'What's her name?' asked Karlene.

'Louise. Louise Webb.'

'Bella reckons she fancies you like mad.'

'Louise isn't like that.'

'So why are you taking her out tomorrow?'

'We're just having a quiet drink together, that's all.'

'One thing leads to another,' joked Karlene.

'Stop teasing him,' said Suzie.

'Louise is a nice girl,' said Mark with quiet affection. 'We enjoy talking to each other.'

'That's how it usually starts.'

'Karlene!' warned Suzie, giving her friend a playful prod.

'We're just friends,' he said. 'We're in the same year and we've got...a lot in common. But that's it, Karlene. We're not an item.'

'Bella thinks you could be.'

Suzie got up. 'Bella thinks about nothing else but pairing people off. She's tried to push me into the arms of some really dreadful guys. Now, go to bed and leave Mark alone.'

She waved good-night as she went upstairs.

'Sorry if I embarrassed you,' said Karlene.

Mark shrugged. 'That's OK.'

'It's just a bit unusual, that's all. As a rule, you don't let any girl come between you and your work. When your head's not buried in a textbook, you goggle at the telly.' She grinned. 'Now you've got something nicer to goggle at — Louise.'

'We're good mates,' he insisted. 'Nothing more.'

But Karlene wasn't fooled. She could see the smile playing around the edges of his mouth. Tomorrow night was a big event in Mark's life. Louise Webb was the first girl he'd shown any real interest in since he'd been at the hospital.

Karlene as pleased for him. Mark seemed hooked.

———————∧∿———————

It was well over an hour before they met Adam's parents. Doctor Minton let them use his office so they could talk in private.

'How is he?' said Bella, anxiously.

'In a disgusting state,' snapped Judith Green.

'Adam's stable,' said her husband in a calmer tone. 'He's still unconscious but the worst is over.'

'Until the next time!' said his wife.

'There won't be a next time, Judith.'

'How often have I heard that?' She turned and looked out of the window.

Gordy and Bella were surprised when they saw Adam's parents. Adam himself looked like a drop-out from a broken home but his parents were smart and well-spoken. They were also older than they'd expected — they were both in their early sixties. Philip Green was a mild man with a serious look about him but his wife had a more spikey manner. She was a handsome woman with beautifully-groomed hair.

Bella found herself blushing under the woman's supercilious stare.

'So you're the new girlfriend, are you?' she said.

'We hardly know Adam,' Gordy interjected. 'We just happened to be at the disco when he collapsed. Bella insisted on coming to the hospital with him. Nobody else would have bothered.'

'We're very grateful to you both,' said Mr Green with a conciliatory smile. 'And we're sorry you've been put to all this inconvenience.'

His wife snorted. '*Underworld*!'

'We were having fun until all this happened,' said Bella.

'Why do you young people go to such dreadful places?' said the woman.

'We like them, Mrs Green,' said Bella, hotly.

'You'll probably end up like Adam, if you're not careful,' she said.

'We are careful,' said Gordy, firmly. 'We're both students here at the hospital so we don't need any lectures about drugs, thank you.'

The woman was slightly taken aback. She sniffed and looked away again. Her husband smiled weakly.

'Please forgive my wife,' he said, softly. 'This has been a great shock to us. We were both asleep when they rang. It's been very distressing.'

'Yes,' agreed Bella. 'It's been a bit alarming for us, too.'

'I can't thank you enough for your concern,' said Mr Green. 'But we'll cope now. Adam's our responsibility. He'll pull through somehow. You two must be exhausted - why don't you get off home now?'

'Great idea!' said Gordy. 'Good-night.'

'Maybe it is time to go,' added Bella. 'Well... Goodbye.'

Mr Green went with them to the door but his wife's voice stopped them; she was staring straight at them, unseeing.

'Sarah,' she said. 'That's when it all started. I'm sure of it. With Sarah.'

'Adam's ex-girlfriend,' explained Mr Green.

'Sarah was good for him,' his wife went on. 'She kept him on an even keel. This wouldn't have happened if Sarah had been around.'

'Possibly not,' said Philip Green, trying to hide his discomfort. 'But it's no use worrying about that now, Judith.'

'Sarah was the right sort of girl for him.' She looked disparagingly at Bella. 'She wasn't the kind of girl to be picked up by anyone at the nearest disco.'

Bella was insulted. 'What did you say?'

'It's definitely time to go,' said Gordy.

'All I did was to dance with Adam,' said Bella.

'So you say,' retorted Judith Green.

'Are you calling me a liar!' Bella was furious now.

'Of course not,' soothed Mr Green, stepping between the two of them. 'Ignore my wife, Bella. She's a little over-wrought. We've been sitting at Adam's bedside, praying he'll recover soon. It's got Judith really upset.'

'Me too, Mr Green,' said Bella, vehemently. 'I was the one in the middle of it all. Do you know what it was like in that disco? Chaos! It's a miracle Adam wasn't trampled to death.' She turned to his wife. 'As for you, Mrs Green, I appreciate you're upset, but that doesn't give you the right to be rude to me. I don't even know Adam — I just danced with your son.'

Judith Green glared angrily at her. Her voice was dripping with contempt.

'Adam is not my son,' she said.

CHAPTER THREE

Suzie came round the corner and saw him. The boy was walking along the corridor, opening every door and peering inside. When he reached a trolley, he got down on his hands and knees to look underneath it.

Hearing Suzie's footsteps, he jumped back up.

'Are you looking for something?' she asked.

'Yeah,' he said. 'Donna — my sister.'

'Well, you won't find her under that trolley.'

'Er...no. She's in Rainbow Ward.'

'Oh, she's a patient here, is she?'

'That's right.'

The boy was short and wiry. He had a mass of dark hair and a cheeky face. He was wearing crumpled jeans and a sweatshirt and in his hand was a large carrier bag. Suzie thought he was about nine. He had a mischievous glint in his eye that amused her.

'The children's wards are on the floor below,' she said. 'I'll show you, if you like. Come on.'

He took a step back. 'Do I have to?'

'I thought you wanted to see your sister?'

'Yeah, I do — in a minute.'

Suzie took a closer look at him. He shifted his feet uneasily. She began to wonder what he was really doing at the hospital. He certainly shouldn't be prying into private rooms.

'What's your name?' she said.

'Tim.'

'And your sister's called Donna?'

'That's right. Donna French. Rainbow Ward.'

'Let me take you down there,' she said, firmly.

Tim looked swiftly up and down the corridor, then walked towards the stairs with her. Suzie could feel his reluctance.

'When was your sister admitted to hospital?'

'Yesterday. But I only came with Mum before. Donna asked me to come today.'

As they reached the staircase Tim French looked back worriedly over his shoulder.

'Have you brought something for your sister?' asked Suzie, glancing down at his bag.

'Oh — it's nothing,' he said, evasively. 'The bag's empty.'

Suzie was getting nowhere. She began to doubt if he really did have a sister in Rainbow Ward. If he had no legitimate reason to be at the hospital, Tim would be told to leave — fast.

She paused as they reached the floor below

'Shouldn't you be at school, Tim?' she asked.

'I sneaked off to see Donna.'

'I don't think you're telling me the truth, are you?' she said.

'Yes, I am,' he said, hotly. He looked past Suzie towards Rainbow Ward. His small face lit up and he pointed.

'Look!' he said. 'There's Donna now!'

Suzie turned round but all she could see were some nurses coming through the double doors. She turned round to Tim — but he was no longer there.

The boy had disappeared into thin air.

—————⋀—————

'I'll never go near that hole again!' said Gordy.

'I don't blame you,' said Karlene. 'It sounds like a real dive. How did Bella come to know this Adam?'

'She doesn't know him, not really. Bel talked to him for a few minutes at *Underworld* last week. Adam's one of those blokes who hangs around on the edges of groups trying to catch your name. Then he claims to be your friend and the next time he sees you, he asks for a favour.'

'Where is he now?' asked Karlene.

'Still here, under observation.'

The two friends had met in the hospital canteen for lunch. Gordy was telling her about the events of the long and exhausting night. Karlene was fascinated.

'What were his parents like?' she said.

'The father was nice. Really embarrassed about his son and even more so about his wife. She was so angry and rude.'

'I'd probably be the same in her position.'

'No, you wouldn't, Kar,' he said. 'You'd care.

Mrs Green didn't seem to care at all. Adam was lying unconscious and all she could think about was herself. Her stepson is dangerously ill.'

'He's her stepson?' asked Karlene.

Gordy nodded. 'Apparently.'

'And what does his father do?'

'He's a headmaster, I think.'

'They always say teachers make the worst parents.'

'Hang on, Kar!' he protested. 'My old man's in education as well. So's Mum. They're great parents. I'm living proof of that.'

'Are you?' said Karlene, grinning. 'Then why've you turned out to be such a mess?' He looked hurt. She changed her tone. 'OK, Gordy. You're the exception to the rule,' said Karlene, trying to smooth his ruffled feathers. 'Your parents have every right to be proud of you. It's obviously not the same with Adam Green.'

Karlene toyed with her food, thinking about what she'd been told. Finally, she decided to give Gordy some advice.

'Stay well clear of him, Gordy,' she said.

'I intend to, Kar.'

'Adam Green sounds like a disaster area. I hope Bella has the sense to do the same.'

'Unfortunately, she doesn't seem to. Bel thinks it's wrong to walk away.'

'Does she feel some sort of obligation?'

'You know Bel,' he said. 'This guy dances with her at a disco, collapses all over her and then almost gets her trampled under foot. What would you do?'

'Run like hell from him,' said Karlene. She became pensive. 'Well, maybe not. It would depend. On whether or not I was in a position to help him.'

'That's a job for the professionals,' said Gordy. 'I tried to get that message through to Bel but she just wouldn't listen. She's gone to visit him. In fact, she's probably sitting at his bedside with a bunch of grapes right this minute.'

Bella had never seen him in daylight before. He looked different. The shadowy figure from the disco was a handsome guy with a pale complexion. He was propped up on pillows. His blue pyjamas matched his eyes. Though he was still drowsy, Adam managed a warm smile.

'Thanks, Bella,' he said.

'For what?'

'Coming here. After what happened, I'm surprised you'd come within a mile of me.'

'I'm more worried about what's actually happened to you.'

He looked puzzled.

'Drugs,' she said.

He was alone in a sideward in the East Wing. Bella knew that it was part of the Rehabilitation

Unit for Drug-Users. It was never short of patients. Drug abuse was widespread in the area. New cases were coming in all the time.

Bella was genuinely concerned about him.

'Didn't you realise the risks you were running?'

'Not until last night.'

'How long have you been taking those pills?'

'That was the first time.'

She was sceptical. 'Adam...'

'It's true, Bella,' he asserted. 'I did a bit of glue-sniffing at school but I hated it. Never even touched Ecstasy until last night. This friend slipped me a few.' He was getting drowsy again and tried to shake himself awake. 'I still don't know what happened. All I can remember is dancing with you.'

'You went wild. Really crazy. I know Ecstasy is supposed to be a stimulant but I didn't know it made you that pumped up.'

'I'm sorry. It must have been horrible for you, Bella. Doctor Minton told me I just crashed out.'

'Yeah, right on top of me.'

He dozed for a second then blinked his eyes open.

'Dad came in to see me this morning,' he said.

'We met your father. And your stepmother.'

'I'm glad he didn't bring her with him.'

'Don't you like her, Adam?'

'She doesn't like me.'

He reached for the jug on his bedside table but

his hand was very unsteady. Bella poured him a glass of water and held it to his lips. He took several sips and nodded his thanks. She felt really sorry for him.

'I hardly know you at all,' she said, changing the subject slightly.

'Me? I'm nobody.'

'You must have a job or something.'

'I used to be a catering student. But I gave it up. Too boring.'

'What are you doing instead, then?'

'Stop interrogating me,' he said, sharply.

'I'm interested, that's all,' said Bella.

'Don't crowd me, Bella.' He was getting upset.

'Sorry.'

Adam's mood seemed to have changed completely. His gentle manner had gone. His eyes started to dart about the room.

'All I want is to get out of this prison!'

Bella could see Adam's resemblance to his father; there were many facial similarities. But unlike Philip Green, he was unpredictable. There was a lot of suppressed bitterness in Adam. Bella remembered the other guy who had come up to Adam at the disco.

'Who's Jez?' she asked. 'The guy who gave you a bit of aggro at *Underworld.*'

'I don't remember.'

'Yes you do. He came up to you when we were dancing.'

'What did he look like?'

'Big and ugly. He threatened to punch you.'

'Oh, that Jez!' he said, slowly identifying the youth. 'He's always heavy.'

'Is he a friend of yours?'

'No way!'

'He seemed to know you pretty well.'

'Everyone knows me at *Underworld*. I get around.'

'He was trying to get something from you, Adam. What was it? What did Jez want?'

'I don't know,' he said, — he clearly could remember nothing. 'A fight, probably. He's always been funny like that.'

He looked drowsy again and his eyes closed suddenly. Bella waited a few minutes until he was fully asleep. Then she began to tiptoe away. Adam woke with a start.

'Don't go,' he begged.

'I have to get back, Adam.'

'You can spare a few more minutes.' He put a hand on her arm. 'This place frightens me.'

'I should let you rest.'

But when she tried to leave, his hand tightened its grasp.

'Don't let her see me like this, Bella — Judith. She'll use it against me. She'll try to get Dad to kick me out of the house. That's what she really wants.'

'But why would she want that?' asked Bella.

'Because I rock the boat. She despises me. She hates me and everything about me. She can't stand any of my friends. She won't even have them in the house.'

'But she did say some nice things about one of your friends.'

'Who was that?'

'Sarah, I think she said.'

Adam looked stunned — it was if she'd just slapped his face. His breathing quickened and his eyes flashed. He struggled to sit up in bed.

'Sarah! She talked about Sarah to you?'

'Mrs Green only mentioned her name.'

'What did she tell you?'

'Only that she liked her.'

'She hardly knew Sarah!'

'She said Sarah had been good for you.'

Adam's breathing got shallower — he started to gasp. His hands began to shake and his head moved rapidly from side to side. He trembled violently. He was getting extremely distressed and agitated — his eyes began to roll upwards. Bella was horrified.

CHAPTER FOUR

Mark found her in the library. Louise Webb had given up her lunch hour to do some work. Like Mark, she was a keen student nurse with real commitment to the course. It was one of the things which had drawn them together.

'Hi, Louise,' he whispered.

'Oh.' She looked up with a smile. 'Hi, Mark.'

'I was hoping to see you in the canteen.'

'I'm not hungry. Besides, I wanted to fit in an extra hour's work. This morning's lecture on care plans inspired me. I slipped in here so I could explore the subject more fully.'

'That's great.'

Mark beamed at her. He'd seen Louise almost every day since the beginning of term and had always found her attractive. But in the last week that attraction had somehow become stronger. It was as if he was looking at her properly for the first time.

Louise was small and slim with auburn hair brushed back from her face. It was her smile that turned Mark on. Her whole face glowed with happiness.

'Are we still on for this evening?' she asked.

'Of course!'

'Where shall we go?'

'Leave it to me,' said Mark.

'I'll do just that,' she said.

Her smile made his heart miss a beat. He couldn't understand it. When he was at school, he'd had girlfriends but they'd been easy-going relationships. There was none of this intense emotion he experienced with Louise. As he gazed down at her now, he couldn't believe he'd plucked up the courage to ask her out.

Louise glanced down at her notes — then became serious.

'Have you made up your mind yet?' she asked. 'About which course you're going to take?'

'That's over a year away,' he said. 'We still have to work our way through the Common Foundation Programme.'

'It doesn't hurt to think about it. Bella says she prefers nursing children.'

'That appeals to me as well.'

'I'd rather specialise in Mental Health,' Louise said.

'It'd be a big challenge,' said Mark, earnestly.

'I'm not afraid of hard work, Mark.'

'No,' he said, fondly. 'You put the rest of us to shame. Nobody on the course works as hard as you do.'

'Only because Sister Killeen cracks the whip over me.'

'She cracks the whip over Bella as well but it doesn't seem to have any effect at all.'

They laughed. Mark basked in the glow of her smile. He wanted to pay her a compliment but he was still too shy with her. Louise made him tongue-tied. He hoped he'd have more confidence when they were out on their first date.

'By the way,' she said, 'what's wrong with Bella? She's so full of life as a rule. But this morning she looked quite pale. Late night?'

'Very late,' said Mark. 'She and Gordy went to the new disco in Wilson Road. *Underworld.*'

'I've heard it's a bit of a dive.'

'Bella danced with a guy who collapsed all over her. On drugs, apparently. They had to call an ambulance. Bella spent hours just sitting in the waiting room at Casualty.'

'No wonder she's whacked.' Louise frowned with concern. 'We won't go there, I hope. To *Underworld*, I mean.'

'No,' he promised her. 'I'd never take you anywhere like that, Louise. I just want to be alone with you.'

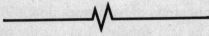

'Then he had this sort of fit,' said Bella. 'It was terrifying.'

'What did you do?'

'I called the nurse at once,' said Bella. 'She put her arms round Adam and held him until the spasm stopped and he'd calmed down. Then she called the doctor in. I wasn't allowed to stay, of course.'

Gordy had finished another day at medical school and had found her waiting for him in the hall. Bella was anxious to give him a progress report on her visit to Adam. She was still very shaken by everything that had happened.

'He seemed fine when I first arrived,' she said.

'I warned you not to go there.'

'But I had to. I feel involved — don't you see?'

'It's nothing to do with you, Bel. You're not being paid to nurse him.'

'But I'm his friend.'

'On the strength of a two-minute dance at a disco?'

They came out of the building and crossed the car park. Bella was clearly upset by his attitude. He slipped an arm around her shoulder.

'I don't mean to sound callous,' he said, 'but you have to put yourself first sometimes. He'll only drag you down with him, Bel. He's the type who latches on to people. Break free while you can.'

'But I can't desert him now. He's really suffering.'

'Adam Green is a drug addict.' Gordy spelt it out.

'No, he's not,' she argued. 'He told me that last night was the first time he'd touched drugs.'

'Come off it, Bel!'

'I believe him.'

'Then you'll fall for anything,' said Gordy, scornfully. 'You only had to look in his eyes to see he was on something. And drugs are not his only problem.'

'What do you mean?'

'Adam is a nutter.'

'That's a terrible thing to say.'

'Maybe, but it's true. He's very disturbed. That's why they've kept him in the Rehab Unit?'

'So that he can recover from last night.'

'That's not the reason, Bel. It's because they want to work on him. Try to wean him off drugs. That means he'll be having sessions with a psychologist. If last night was a one-off mistake, why would they be giving him treatment?'

'I don't know,' she admitted. 'They probably want to evaluate him, that's all.'

'They have evaluated him, Bel. He's crazy.'

'Stop saying that!'

She pushed his arm away and swung round to confront him. They were standing in the middle of the car park now.

'Adam desperately needs someone on his side right now.'

'He's got his parents.'

'His father, maybe. But his stepmother really dislikes him.'

'Mrs Green dislikes most people, by the look of her. But listen to me, Bel. Stay out of it.'

'I can't, I just can't,' she said.

'What more does he have to do to scare you off?' said Gordy with sarcasm. 'He collapsed on top of you at the disco. He has some kind of hysterical fit in front of you here. Next time, he'll turn into a werewolf and chase you all over the building.'

'It's not funny!' she protested.

'Anyone else would have been put off by what happened just now.'

'But I helped to cause it. I did, Gordy. It happened when I mentioned Sarah's name.'

'Was Sarah the girl his stepmother went on about?'

'That's right,' she said. 'I've no idea why her name upset him so much but it's one more reason why I can't just turn my back on him. I really want to know who Sarah is and why she has such an effect on him?' Bella smiled. 'It's not just sympathy for Adam. I'm curious.'

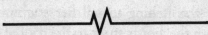

Mark brought the drinks across to the table and sat opposite her. Louise surprised him. He'd expected her to ask for a glass of wine but she ordered lager. The pub was close to the hospital and quiet that early in the evening. They could chat freely. There was a faint buzzing sound in Mark's ears. He soon forgot it.

'Cheers!' said Louise, raising her glass.

'Yes,' he responded. 'Cheers!'

They sipped their beer and smiled at each other.

'Have you been here before?' she said.

'Once or twice — with Bella and Gordy.'

'Bella's really lively, isn't she?'

'She never stops.'

'Isn't it a bit exhausting living with her?'

'Bella's not there most of the time,' said Mark. 'She has rather a busy social life.'

Louise sipped her beer and studied him over the rim of her glass. The faintest hint of jealousy crept in.

'Do you fancy her, Mark?'

'Of course, not!'

'Every other guy in our year does.'

'I'm not every other guy.'

'She's very attractive.'

'But she's just not my type, Louise.'

'Then who is?'

Mark was itching to tell her she was his ideal woman but the words stuck to the roof of his mouth again. He had a quick drink to give himself some courage. It was their first date and he was very cautious.

'Anyway,' he said, eventually. 'It's just not on. Suzie made that clear from the start. No close relationships. Five of us share that house. If any two of us became an "item", it would upset the whole balance. Bella can never be more than a friend.'

Louise was reassured. She looked serious. 'Has it come as a big shock to you?' she said. 'Nursing?'

'Not really.'

'It has to me,' she confided. 'For the first few weeks I was in a complete daze. Running around in small circles with Sister Killeen yelling at me. I kept asking what I'd let myself in for.'

'And now?'

'Well, now I've got used to it. Weren't you put off at first?'

'No, Louise. I've always loved it.'

'Even emptying the bedpans?'

'I try to look the other way,' he grinned.

'If you do that, you spill the contents. I got my feet soaked the first time.' They laughed and compared other disasters that had happened to them both. 'What about the unsocial hours?' she said.

'No problem.' He risked a tentative compliment. 'Especially if I was on night duty with you.'

Louise gave him an encouraging smile. He began to relax. Mark was taking things very slowly, feeling his way through the conversation. She was not a talkative and vivacious girl like Bella. She was much quieter and self-contained - more serious. He found that appealing. The buzzing in his ears grew louder. He shook his head to try and clear it but the sound remained.

'What about the other girls you share with?' she said.

said.

'Suzie and Karlene?'

'Do you fancy either of them?'

'No,' he said, quickly. 'That doesn't even come into it. We just...get along well together.'

'So there's been nobody since you've been here?'

He shook his head. 'No. What about you?'

'I've had offers,' she said, smiling. 'But it wasn't all that difficult to turn them down.'

'You didn't turn me down,' he managed to say.

'No, I didn't, did I?'

With another smile, she slipped off her coat and let it hang on the back of the chair. She was wearing a white silk shirt with a black mini-skirt. Mark was pleased she'd dressed up for the evening. He'd put on his best denim shirt and Levis but he still felt dowdy beside her.

He finally said what he was really thinking.

'You look great, Louise.'

'Thanks, Mark.'

'But then you always do.'

'You should see me first thing in the morning!'

He laughed nervously with embarrassment. Then he shook his head again, trying to get rid of the buzzing sound that was still troubling him.

Louise put her elbows on the table and leant forward.

'Why haven't we done this before?' she said.

'I don't know.'

'I noticed you looking at me in lectures.'

'I couldn't keep my eyes off you, Louise,' he confessed. 'You're the best student on the course. And the most attractive. I really wanted to ask you out but I was afraid you'd turn me down.'

'Not a chance!' she said. 'I was praying you'd get round to it in the end and you did. You're not like the other guys on the course, Mark. They come on too strong. Not you. And I feel I can talk to you. And the wonderful thing is you listen.'

Mark was delighted. His nervousness faded away. He sensed this was going to be the best evening since he'd come to the hospital. He intended to savour every moment of it.

But as he lifted his drink, he had a momentary dizzy spell. The glass fell from his hand and smashed to pieces on the table. Fragments were thrown all over Louise along with most of his beer.

She looked down at her sodden clothes in total disbelief.

'Oh, no!' she exclaimed. 'You're so clumsy, Mark! You've ruined my new shirt.'

Mark felt mortified and Louise burst into tears.

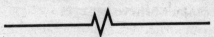

Living so close to the hospital had many advantages. Suzie was able to slip home to change out of her uniform. It was her tutor's birthday and she was going to a surprise drinks party for her in the lecture room. When her tutor left her office at seven o'clock, she would be met by a gang of her students. They wanted to celebrate her birthday in style.

It took all their skill to keep the party a secret but she didn't mind the effort. Suzie was very fond of her tutor and glad of the chance to show it. Walking back to the hospital, she went into the main block and headed for the stairs. Unless she was in a hurry, she rarely took the lift. Climbing stairs was good exercise. It helped to build up stamina.

When she reached the second floor, she paused to look across at Rainbow Ward. Suzie remembered her meeting with Tim. His sudden disappearance still mystified her. She toyed with the idea of going to see if Donna French really was a patient there but she had no time. She had to be in the lecture room before seven. They all wanted the party to be a complete surprise for their tutor.

Suzie ran up the last flight of stairs in a happy mood. But when she raised her head, she saw something that made her stop in her tracks. Sitting on the top step, watching her with intense curiosity, was a large, white rabbit.

She couldn't believe her eyes.

CHAPTER FIVE

Gordy poured milk over his breakfast cereal. A late night had left him feeling rather weary. He spooned food into his mouth and chewed it absently.

'What do you think?' asked Karlene.

'I think she was drunk.'

'This was before the party. Suzie hadn't touched a drop.'

'If she saw a white rabbit, she'd been boozing.'

'Suzie swears she was stone cold sober.'

'Then she was on hallucinogenic drugs.'

'You know her better than that,' said Karlene. 'She doesn't make up stories. If Suzie says she saw a white rabbit at the hospital, then I believe her.'

'What did it do — jump out of a magician's hat? She's making it up, Kar.'

'No, I'm not,' said Suzie, coming into the kitchen in her dressing gown. 'It was on the top step. As large as life.'

'With ten pink elephants beside it,' he teased.

'You can mock, Gordy. I know what I saw.'

'Where did the rabbit come from?' asked Karlene.

'I've no idea.'

'An over-heated imagination maybe?' suggested Gordy, ducking Suzie's raised hand.

'I've no idea where it vanished to, either,' said Suzie. 'One second it was on the step then —

whoosh! Away!'

'Straight back to Alice in Wonderland!' he said.

'Oh shut up, Gordy,' scolded Karlene. 'I want to hear this. What did you do, Suzie?'

'At first I thought I'd flipped.'

'Didn't you report it to security?'

'I had a party to rush off to,' said Suzie. 'Besides, I didn't think security would take me seriously if I reported sighting a white rabbit. They'd just snigger like Gordy.'

'I'm not sniggering, Suze,' he said. 'I just know you couldn't have seen a white rabbit. A brown one, maybe. There are dozens of them all over the hospital. Squirrels, too. I've even spotted a herd of goats in Reception.'

Suzie gave him a playful slap on the arm and went to make herself some coffee. There was no point in trying to have a serious discussion about her strange encounter when Gordy was around.

'What've you got today, Karlene?' she asked.

'Fractures.'

'That should be interesting.'

'We're going to watch some physios working with patients who've had compound fractures. You know, helping them to get full mobility back.'

'What about you, Gordy?'

'We're going on a big game hunt for white rabbits.'

Karlene waved her fork at him. 'I'll prong you if

48

you don't stop teasing her. Suzie asked a question.'

'The answer is Anatomy.'

'I'm observing in the X-ray Department again,' said Suzie. 'The radiographers make it look so easy but it's not. Then I'm having lunch with Bella.'

Gordy became serious. 'Good. Then maybe you can talk her out of it - her obsession with Adam Green.'

'She seems to think he needs her,' said Karlene.

Suzie nodded. 'That's what Bella told me. She feels tied into his case. Even though she hardly knows him.'

'Adam's bad news,' said Gordy. 'Get that message across to her.'

'It's Bella's decision,' reminded Karlene.

'He freaked out in the Rehab Unit yesterday.'

'Maybe that was the result of coming off drugs,' said Suzie. 'You know, withdrawal symptoms.'

Gordy was adamant. 'It's Bella who should be showing withdrawal symptoms. Withdrawal from Adam Green. She'll regret it otherwise. And we'll feel guilty that we didn't step in and rescue her.'

'Bella insists she must help him,' said Karlene.

'He's beyond help.'

'Stay out of it, Gordy,' she advised. 'Let Bella do what she wants. She's going to be a nurse, remember. A good one. Bella has all the right instincts.'

Gordy gave up and returned grumpily to his breakfast. Suzie made her coffee then made some toast. Karlene looked up as she heard water gushing out of the bath.

'Bella's finished at last. My turn next.'

'Be quick,' said Suzie, 'or Mark'll beat you to it.'

Karlene shook her head. 'No, he won't. Mark was up at the crack of dawn. I heard him leave the house.'

'Maybe he's got an early date with Louise,' said Gordy.

'I doubt it,' said Karlene. 'I was here when he got back last night. He looked dreadful. That romance seems to have crumbled before it got going.'

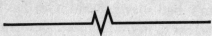

Mark stood in front of the department store in the light drizzle. Several shirts were on display in the window. His date with Louise had been a wash-out. His only hope of making amends was to replace the silk shirt he'd ruined by his carelessness. He cheered up when he spotted a shirt almost identical to the one Louise had been wearing. Then he saw the price.

'Fifty quid!' he groaned. 'I can't afford that on my grant.'

He walked away — dejected.

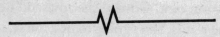

'I thought you'd still be in bed,' said Bella in surprise.

'It's much nicer in here.'

'You're not even wearing pyjamas.'

'They let me put my clothes back on,' said Adam, smiling.

'You look so much better Adam.'

'I feel it.'

Bella had agonised a long time before making a second visit to Adam. The meeting in the side ward had been traumatic. She was anxious to avoid any repetition of that. And Bella knew it might be dangerous to develop any kind of relationship with him.

But her curiosity was greater than her fear. She was keen to learn more about him. She wanted to understand what made him tick. Something about him made her like Adam. Deep down, she felt she could reach him in ways that others might not be able to.

They had met in the recreation room on the third floor. Other patients were playing cards together, reading magazines or chatting in small groups. Adam led her to a couple of armchairs by a window. They looked out on a panoramic view of the city.

'I never thought I'd see you again, Bella,' he said.

'Why not?'

'Because of what happened yesterday.'

'I think that was my fault.'

'Don't be silly,' he said. 'It was nothing to do with you. The doctor explained it to me. Those drugs I took at *Underworld* left me all tensed up.

Even though I'd had my stomach pumped, the drugs were still affecting me. I wasn't in control.'

'Yes, but I triggered the attack.'

'No, you didn't. I'm the one who should apologise. All you did was show an interest in me. And I flip. It must have been a bit of a shock for you.'

'It was,' she confessed. 'But I'm pleased you seem so much better now.'

'I am, Bella. Completely.'

Adam was transformed. The drowsy person he'd been on her previous visit was now friendly and alert. He'd just had a bath and his hair was brushed down on his head. Bella could see just how good-looking he really was. There didn't seem any sign of any physical or mental problems. He seemed perfectly normal. Bella was reassured.

'So what's the next step?' she asked.

He grinned. 'Escape!'

'Has the doctor said anything yet?'

'He's keeping me in for a while - then he wants me to attend a clinic here as an outpatient.'

'Why's that?' asked Bella.

'For drug counselling.'

'But you told me you only took Ecstasy that once,' she reminded him. 'I thought the clinic was for real addicts. Heroin-users, mainly.'

'Yes,' he conceded. 'It is.'

'So where do you fit in?'

Adam shrugged. 'They just want to scare me,

Bella. Put me off drugs for good by showing me what happens when you get totally addicted. But I've already had a big enough scare. That's it. No more fooling around.'

'Do you mean that, Adam?'

'I swear it!'

Bella believed him. He was obviously sincere. Now he'd recovered from his collapse, he wanted to put the whole incident behind him and start afresh. He was hoping she might be involved in that fresh start.

'Thanks, Bella,' he said, softly.

'I wanted to see you.'

'You're the only person who does. Except Dad.'

'Has he been in today?'

'Not yet.'

'He'll be amazed at the improvement.'

'I've let him down badly,' sighed Adam. 'And I played right into Judith's hands. She'll make Dad suffer for this. She'll nag him to death about what a useless son he's got.'

'Do you have any brothers or sisters?' asked Bella.

'No, I'm an only child,' he said.

Bella was wary about probing any further. Though keen to learn more about his family, she didn't want to provoke another attack. Adam seemed calm and confident now but she hadn't forgotten the spasm which had seized him the day before. He needed gentle handling.

Suddenly, he looked defensive. 'We are friends, aren't we?' he said.

'Of course.'

'You're not just here because you feel sorry for me?'

'No, Adam.'

He took a deep breath. 'Can I tell you something? Do you know why I asked you to dance at *Underworld*?'

'You were chatting me up.'

'There was more to it than that,' he said, biting his lip. 'The truth is you reminded me of her—Sarah. It was uncanny. And then when you mentioned her name yesterday...'

His voice trailed away and he was lost in thought for a few minutes. Bella didn't dare interrupt him. She waited patiently until he noticed her again.

'Sorry,' he said. 'I was miles away.'

'With Sarah?'

'Don't ever talk about her again,' he pleaded. 'It's too painful, Bella. I can't bear to think about it. Let's talk about you instead.'

He squeezed her hand gently. Bella felt uncomfortable but did her best not to show it. She was ready to be friends with Adam but she certainly didn't want a more intimate relationship. She was still very conscious of how little she really knew about him.

Bella gave him a smile and rose to leave.

'I'll have to get back now, I'm afraid. Or she'll kill me.'

'Who?'

'Sister Killeen. Our tutor.'

'Will you come again?' he said. 'Please.'

'If you're still here.'

'I will be, Bella. Waiting for you.'

He stood up and walked to the door with her. She was afraid he might try to kiss her but he simply nodded his thanks and waved goodbye as she left. Bella had plenty to think about as she went down in the lift. Though she was glad to see him looking so much better, she was a little disturbed by his interest in her.

Sarah had obviously been very important in his life. Bella wondered what it was about her that reminded him of his former girlfriend.

She was still thinking it over when she walked into Reception. When she saw the rangy figure at the desk, he looked vaguely familiar. As he turned round, she got a closer look at him; his face was pock-marked, his hair cropped short. His wild eyes darted everywhere.

Bella had only seen him once before and that had been in the subdued light of the disco. But she recognised him instantly. It was Jez. He'd butted in on their dancing and argued with Adam. Jez frightened her — there was a sense of danger about him.

When his hostile stare fixed on her, she felt sick.

CHAPTER SIX

There was something odd about the woman. Karlene couldn't work out what it was. Of all the patients she saw that day, Virginia Tyc was by far the most interesting. Her arm had been fractured in three places and she'd been in plaster for a long time. Now the cast was removed, she was being helped by physiotherapy to regain full use of her arm.

Karlene was one of the students watching. As the session came to an end, most of her friends lingered in the room. She wandered out and strolled across to the lift. Mrs Tyc was waiting there on her own. She was wearing a headscarf now. She smiled nervously at Karlene.

'How do you feel now, Mrs Tyc?' she said.

'Much better, thanks.'

'Did that massage help?'

'A lot. My arm was very stiff at first.'

'It's not surprising. How did you break it?'

'I slipped and fell in the kitchen,' said the woman.

Virginia Tyc was slim and of medium height - probably in her late twenties. But the anxiety in her face made her seem much older. Her eyes looked haunted, her movements nervous and jerky. And Karlene wondered why she wore so much heavy make-up.

'I'm Karlene Smith, by the way,' she said.

'Hello.'

'Your name's unusual — where's it from?' asked Karlene.

'It's Polish. My husband is from Gdansk. But I was born in Bedford.'

'Not too far from me, then. I come from Luton.'

Mrs Tyc gave her a brief smile. She appeared eager to get away and was pleased when the lift finally arrived. Karlene had never met anyone so defensive. They got into the empty lift together and pressed the button for the ground floor.

'Sorry you had to put up with us,' she said. 'Students, goggling at you.'

'Oh...I didn't mind.'

'We have to learn somehow. But I know it can feel intrusive.'

Virginia Tyc pulled the edges of her headscarf forward. When she'd done that, she seemed to relax a little and looked at Karlene properly for the first time.

'I've got to pick up my children now,' she said.

'How many do you have?'

'Two — they're twins. They're at playgroup.'

'What do they speak at home? English or Polish?' asked Karlene, trying to show an interest.

But the question seemed to alarm the woman. She looked around furtively, tugging at her headscarf. Karlene was immediately apologetic.

'I didn't mean to be nosy, Mrs Tyc. It's really none of my business.'

'Both,' said the woman, suddenly. The lift reached the ground floor and the doors opened. 'English, mostly. But my husband's teaching them Polish as well.'

'I wish I could speak another language.'

'Excuse me. I've got to go. The children are waiting.'

'Don't let me hold you up.'

'Goodbye.'

'Bye, Mrs Tyc.'

Karlene stepped aside to let the woman out into Reception. Sunshine flooded in through the main windows. It struck the side of Mrs Tyc's face and revealed something Karlene hadn't noticed before — one of her cheeks was swollen.

That explained the heavy make-up and the headscarf pulled carefully over her face. Neither could completely hide the injury.

She had a large and ugly bruise.

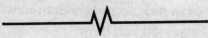

'What do you think he was doing here?' asked Suzie.

'I don't know,' said Bella. 'I just hope he wasn't looking for Adam. Jez is a real hard case. The last thing Adam needs right now is someone like that barging in on him.'

'Are you quite sure it was him?'

'Oh yes. It was Jez all right. He's scary.'

'Adam seems to hang out with some weird people.'

'Jez isn't a friend — just an acquaintance.'

'Be careful, anyway,' warned Suzie. 'You don't want to get mixed up with creeps like that.'

They'd finished their lunch in the canteen then gone their separate ways. Suzie was interested to hear about Bella's second visit to East Wing. As a rule, she only ever talked about her latest boyfriend. It was a pleasant change to find her in a more serious mood. In spite of what had happened, she seemed committed to helping Adam. Suzie was impressed.

With part of her lunch break still left, she took the opportunity to go to Rainbow Ward. Her strange meeting with Tim French still troubled her. Was his sister really a patient at the hospital or had the boy been lying?

The ward sister quickly dispelled part of the mystery.

'Yes,' she said. 'We do have a Donna French here.'

'Have they diagnosed her condition yet?'

'I can't discuss the patient's case, I'm afraid. It's confidential.'

'Of course not,' said Suzie.

'Would it be possible to see Donna, though?'

'If you want to come back during Visiting

Hours, certainly.'

'I couldn't have five minutes with her now, could I?'

'I'm afraid not,' said the sister.

She was pleasant but firm. She wouldn't allow unauthorised people to wander around her ward even if they were students at the hospital. Suzie had to accept that.

She was just walking away when she heard panting sounds. Somebody was racing up the stairs. Suzie waited to see who would appear. A tousled head came into view. Tim French was taking the steps two at a time.

When he saw Suzie, he stopped guiltily. He was gasping for breath after his energetic climb up the stairs. He was wearing the same clothes as the day before but was carrying a sports bag with the name and crest of Manchester United on it.

'Hi, Tim,' she said with a friendly smile.

'Hello,' he grunted.

'What happened to you yesterday? You distracted me and then ran off.'

'I had somewhere to go.'

'It must have been somewhere very important, then.'

'Did you find what you were looking for?'

Tim said nothing. He was still suspicious of her. Because she wore a uniform, he assumed she was part of the hospital staff and that meant she'd try to stop him.

'What are you doing here?' Suzie asked.

'I've come to see Donna.'

'They won't let you in outside Visiting Time,' she told him.

'Yes they will — I'm family. We can come whenever we likes.'

Suzie felt a surge of sympathy. Visiting hours in the children's wards were more flexible than elsewhere. Sick children needed extra reassurance when they were separated from their families. Parents often stayed the whole day at the hospital and even stayed overnight.

But only patients who were seriously ill could have unrestricted visiting hours. If Donna French's brother could come and go at will, she must be very sick.

'Is Donna in a sideward?' asked Suzie. 'On her own?'

'That's right.'

'And they still don't know what's wrong with her?'

He shook his head. 'They got her on this machine.'

Tim had run a long way. Sweat was streaming down his face. He put down his bag and used his arm to wipe his forehead. Suzie was touched by his devotion to his sister.

'Did you sneak off school again?' she said.

'Yeah — only in me lunch hour.'

'And you'll have to run all the way back as well then?'

'I don't mind,' said Tim.

'I won't delay you, then,' said Suzie as she stepped aside. 'Go in and see Donna.'

'Have you brought something for her?' said Suzie, glancing down at the sports bag with a smile. It soon froze on her face. The bag was moving from side to side — she was mesmerised. It seemed to be alive.

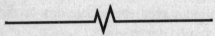

It was a most frustrating day for Mark. Desperate to be alone with Louise, he just couldn't find the right moment. She was always with someone. He believed she was doing it deliberately in order to avoid him. Whenever their eyes met, she gave him a guarded smile. The ruined silk shirt still annoyed her.

Mark wasn't helped by the fact that he felt a cold coming. His throat tickled and he was starting to sneeze. But he was determined not to leave until he'd made his peace with Louise. He lurked in the entrance hall at the end of the day in the hope of catching her as she left. After rehearsing his apology for the hundredth time, he was foiled once again. When Louise finally appeared, she had someone with her. What made it worse was that her companion was Bella.

The two of them were locked in conversation.

'They do such important work there,' said Louise. 'Every hospital ought to have a Drug Rehabilitation Unit like ours. Why don't they?'

'There's an easy answer to that, Louise. Lack of money. The NHS is starved of resources. Running a Rehab Unit is expensive. There are doctors, psychologists and nursing staff involved, as well as social workers. Adam's lucky to be here.'

'Yes,' agreed Louise. 'It must be fascinating for you, getting an insight into how the Unit works. I envy you.'

'All I've done is visit one patient.'

'Yes, but he wouldn't be in there unless his case was an acute one. Has he been screened by a psychologist yet? That's the side of it I'm really interested in, you see. Mental health.'

'There's nothing wrong with Adam's mental health.'

'Drugs can have strange effects on the mind.'

Bella bit back her reply. She felt Louise was making a false assumption about Adam but she didn't want to have an argument. Mark intercepted them.

'Hi, Louise,' he said.

'Hi.'

'You've seen each other all day,' commented Bella. 'Why are you greeting each other as if you'd just met?' She put her hands up and backed quickly away. 'Sorry. You want to be alone. Excuse me.'

As soon as she was gone, Mark tried to speak but he found himself sneezing loudly. He held his handkerchief over his nose.

'Bless you!' said Louise.

'Sorry,' he said, taking a step towards her.

'Don't come too close,' said Louise, backing away slightly. 'I don't want to catch your germs.'

'I'm fine now,' he said, pocketing his handkerchief.

They walked towards the door in silence. The buzzing noise in Mark's ears had returned. As they hit the fresh air, he stifled another sneeze.

'I owe you an apology for last night,' he said.

'Forget it.' Louise brushed it aside.

'But it was such a great shirt.'

'My parents bought it for me,' she said, sadly. 'As a present for getting in here. That's why it was so special.'

'I'll get you another one,' he promised, recklessly.

'Just forget it, will you? The beer stains will come out if I wash it carefully.'

'Let me do that for you, Louise.'

She turned to face him. He could see anger mingled with affection in her face. Mark wanted to take her in his arms but he felt another sneeze rising. He just managed to control it but the buzzing in his ears was more distracting than ever. He made an effort to concentrate.

'Maybe we could have another drink sometime,' he said.

She was non-committal. 'Maybe.'

'This weekend, perhaps?'

'I'm busy. Look, let's not rush things.'

'Does that mean you'd rather I just backed off?'

'It means I'd like some time to sort things out in my mind,' she said, pleasantly. 'It wasn't only the accident with the beer, Mark. The truth is I'm not ready for anything too serious. Not yet, anyway.'

'Fair enough,' he said, disappointed. 'I won't bother you again. As long as we're still friends.'

'Of course,' she said, giving him a kinder smile. 'I'm still mad at you for spilling beer over me but — yes, we're friends.'

Mark felt both saddened and reassured. But there was an unexpected bonus; on impulse, Louise leant towards him and kissed him, gently, on the cheek. Then she swung off across the car park.

Mark was delighted. That one sign of affection wiped away a whole day of misery; Louise still liked him. It was something to build on. He decided to catch up with her and walk her home but his feet rebelled. Instead of running after Louise, he found himself staggering a few paces and leaning on a parked car for support.

Mark was alarmed. He'd completely lost his balance.

CHAPTER SEVEN

Philip Green leapt up from his seat when she came into Reception. He was wearing a dark suit and had a briefcase beside him. Bella went across to shake his hand. He'd rung her at the college of nurses to ask for a meeting.

'Thank you so much for coming,' he began.

'You said it was urgent. Have you been to see Adam?'

'I've just spent an hour with him.' He glanced around. 'Is there somewhere a little more private?'

'Follow me.'

Bella led him out of the hospital and along the main street. They were soon sitting down together in a cafe. Philip Green's face was lined with anxiety.

'I'm so sorry you've got drawn into this, Bella,' he began. 'It must be very distressing for you.'

'I'd just like to see Adam get better. How was he when you visited him just now?'

'Volatile. One moment he seems quite articulate, the next, he's saying all kinds of ridiculous things. The reason I wanted to see you was that he kept bringing up your name. Adam seems to have become quite obsessed with you,' he continued.

'But we've only met a couple of times,' Bella said, looking alarmed.

'That doesn't matter. You've obviously made a

big impression. He talks about you as if you're a close friend. Adam fantasizes — he's already weaving you into his dreams.'

'I see,' said Bella, shifting uneasily in her chair. 'All I can offer him is sympathy, I'm afraid. I'm not up for anything else.'

'I know. That's why I felt I should warn you that Adam may begin to make demands on you.'

Mr Green sipped his cup of tea and looked thoughtful. He was trying to work out how much he should tell Bella. Confiding in her at all was evidently something of an ordeal for him.

'Adam has had a lot of problems,' he admitted. 'I blame myself to some extent. I was never there for him when he really needed me. Then there's my wife...'

'Adam said Mrs Green hated him.'

'I wouldn't put it that strongly, Bella. It's just that...well, he's not the stepson Judith would have chosen. Adam is too wild and independent. He's a maverick.'

'Nothing wrong with that,' she said with a grin. 'I'm one myself.'

'I doubt if you go off the rails quite as often as Adam — or quite as dramatically.' He sighed. 'The simplest thing would be to wash my hands of him. It's certainly what Judith would like. Throw him out and shunt the problem on to someone else.'

'You can't do that to your own son,' protested

Bella. 'He'd really go to pieces then. Don't turn your back on him now, Mr Green.'

'I'm not going to, Bella. But I can't just welcome him home with open arms. The very mention of drugs disgusts Judith. She doesn't want him anywhere near her.'

'Adam only took those pills this once,' insisted Bella.'

'Is that what he told you?' He sighed again. 'Then you've been badly misled. Adam's had a drug problem for over six months. This is the second time he's been admitted to hospital.'

Bella tried to take it all in; she was shocked and angry with herself for being so gullible. She wondered how many other lies Adam had told her.

'Why does he do it, Mr Green?' she asked.

'You tell me.'

'He's got so much going for him.'

'That may be one of the reasons — raising two fingers at everything we believe in. It's soul-destroying, Bella. He just won't listen to us.'

'Has he always been like this?' she asked.

'Far from it — we used to get along quite well. Adam's always had a stubborn streak but he was amiable enough most of the time. Especially when Sarah was around. She was at school with him. Sarah Baker was a lovely girl. They went on to the College of Food and Technology together. Sarah was a good influence on him. They were never apart.'

'So why did it break up?' Bella was fascinated. 'Mrs Green said Adam went downhill after Sarah left.'

'We don't know the true story,' he confessed, 'and neither of us ever will. For some reason, Sarah wanted out. Adam seemed to go to pieces from that point on.'

'It must have been awful for you — watching it happen'

'The drugs have changed him, Bella. He was never moody before, or dishonest.' His face hardened. 'The stealing — that really hurt Judith. He stole money from us to buy drugs.'

'That's dreadful!' Bella was horrified.

'It's been heart-breaking.' He gave her a wan smile. 'You'll understand now why I had to warn you. Adam is very plausible and I don't want you to be fooled like we were at first.'

'Thank you, Mr Green,' said Bella.

She felt profoundly sorry for him. He was in an impossible position; caught between his wife and his son, he would experience a lot more suffering. Bella could see no easy solution. It certainly made her think more critically about her friendship with Adam. She felt quite apprehensive about him now.

'What happened to Sarah?' she asked.

'I wish I knew because she's the one person who might help him,' he said. 'Sarah kept him on the right track. She was really vivacious — a bit like you, in a way.'

'That's what Adam said,' she recalled.

'I've often thought of trying to track her down, to ask her if she'd at least speak to Adam — help straighten him out. If anyone could do it, Sarah could.'

'Then why not ask her?' said Bella.

'Because I don't know where she is. Her parents live nearby on the Mount Pleasant Estate but Sarah's left home. I'm not even sure she's still living in the area.'

Bella could see what an important figure Sarah was in Adam's life. If she could be contacted, she might take some of the burden off Bella herself. At the very least, Sarah could help them understand what had really happened to Adam.

'I'll find her,' she said to herself. 'Somehow.'

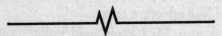

'What did you say her name was?' asked Gordy.

'Mrs Tyc.'

'As in tick-tock, you mean?'

'It's spelt T-Y-C. Her husband's Polish.'

'With a name like that, he has to be a Polish watchmaker.'

'All I know is, his wife seems very afraid of him.'

'Is that what she told you?'

'No,' said Karlene. 'She didn't need to. I guessed it from her manner. She was so nervous.'

'You mean, she had this nervous tick!'

'Gordy!' She jabbed him with her spoon. 'This is important. Can't you take anything seriously?'

They were sitting on the sofa in their living-room. Karlene was eating a yoghurt while he munched an apple. He was not impressed by her theory about Virginia Tyc.

'How do you know it was a bruise on her face?'

'Because I saw it under the make-up.'

'It could have been a birthmark or something.'

'The poor woman was on edge all the time she was with us,' said Karlene. 'She hated having an audience and couldn't wait to rush off. I sensed this deep fear.'

'Maybe she was just shy.'

'It's something to do with her husband,' Karlene persisted.

'Then let her sort it out.'

'You're so callous sometimes.'

'I'm just being practical,' said Gordy. 'You're a physio not a marriage guidance counsellor. Deal with the problem that's in front of you. Don't get dragged into domestic squabbles.'

'Suppose that broken arm was the result of a quarrel?'

'It's still nothing to do with you. Learn your lesson from Bella. She's being sucked into a no-win situation. Don't do the same thing with Mrs Tock.'

'Tyc!'

'Tock. Tick-tock, tick-tock!'

Karlene grabbed a cushion and swung it at him but Gordy jumped out of the way. They heard the key in the lock as Suzie came into the house. Gordy switched his attack.

'Hello, Suze,' he taunted. 'What did you see at the hospital today? Another white rabbit? Or a charging rhino?'

'Ignore him,' said Karlene. 'He's in one of his peculiar moods.'

'Gordy's entitled to an answer,' said Suzie, easily. 'I saw the white rabbit again. At least, I saw what I'm fairly certain was the animal.'

'Where?' asked Karlene.

'Hidden away inside a sports bag.'

'Amazing!' exclaimed Gordy. 'Suze has only been a radiodog for five minutes and she's already got X-ray eyes.'

'It was simple deduction,' she explained. 'That's what the boy was searching for yesterday — his missing rabbit. He'd obviously found it because it was jumping around inside the bag he was carrying.'

'Why do you two have all the fun?' sighed Gordy. 'Kar meets a woman who's been beaten to a pulp by her mad Polish husband and you see invisible white rabbits. All I did was to sit through a boring lecture.'

'What's this about a mad Polish husband?' said Suzie.

Karlene shrugged. 'A theory I have about a patient.'

'Spare me the re-run,' said Gordy. 'I'll cook the meal while you fill Suzie in with the details.' He saw a figure go past the window. 'That's good timing. Here's Mark.'

When Mark let himself into the house, he looked rather pale. He was so preoccupied that he hardly noticed the others. Gordy waved a hand in front of Mark's face, to no effect. He snapped his fingers and Mark came out of his reverie. He waved a belated greeting at them.

'How do you get beer stains out of a silk shirt?' he said.

They all three burst into laughter — Mark couldn't understand why. As Gordy went off to prepare the supper, they heard pots and pans banged noisily.

'How many am I cooking for?' he asked. 'Four or five?'

'Four,' said Mark. 'Bella got delayed.'

'Don't tell me she's gone to see Adam again!'

'Not him, Gordy - his father. My guess is, she won't be back for some time.'

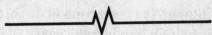

They walked back to the hospital so that Philip Green could spend some more time with his son. Bella went into Reception with him and crossed to the lift. The discussion had opened her eyes. She not only saw Adam as a cunning liar, she realised just how gullible she'd been. She would never be quite so trusting again.

'Goodbye, Bella,' he said, shaking her hand.

'Bye, Mr Green. And thanks for the warning.'

She waited until the lift doors closed after him then turned to walk towards the entrance. A rangy figure blocked her way. It was Jez. She stopped dead in her tracks.

'What do you want?' she said.

'It was you, wasn't it?' he snarled. 'It was you at the disco with Adam the other night.'

'Maybe.'

'The nurse's uniform threw me at first. Then I seen you with his old man, Mr Green. So I put two and two together. Clever? They won't let me see Adam,' he complained.

'That's good news!' said Bella, defiantly.

'I can't get to him — but you can.'

'Please — move out of my way,' she said.

'Deliver a message for me. Tell him it's from Jez.'

He was towering over her in the most menacing way. Bella looked around for a security guard but no one was in sight. Jez put a hand under her chin and forced her to look into his wild eyes.

'I want my money!' he hissed. 'Got it? Tell Adam I want my money. Now. Or he's in big trouble!'

Aspirins and an early night seemed to have done the trick. Mark felt much better. His head had cleared and the tickle had vanished from his throat. When he got out of bed, there was no hint of the dizziness he'd been feeling recently.

It was only half-past six but he was keen to start the new day. He decided that the situation with Louise might not be as bad as he'd feared. She was at least talking to him again. As long as we're still friends, he thought, there's hope.

When he came downstairs, he expected to find the place in darkness but there was a light on in the kitchen. Bella was slumped over an empty mug at the table. Mark was astonished. She was usually one of the last to get up.

'Morning, Bella.'

'Oh. Hi, Mark,' she said, dully.

'You feeling all right?' She nodded. 'What can I get you? Tea, coffee, orange, juice?'

'Anything'll do.'

He poured two glasses of orange juice and sat opposite her. She gave him a half-smile of thanks. It was rare to find Bella in such an introspective mood. He guessed why.

'Is it that guy you met at the disco?' he said.

She clicked her tongue. 'Yes.'

'What did his father want?'

'To give me a friendly warning, Mark. To tell me a few things about Adam that I didn't know.'

'Such as?'

'That he's disturbed — that he's a compulsive liar, that he's been on drugs for some time and actually stole money from his parents to buy them.' She sighed. 'Honestly, I felt such an idiot. I'd believed everything Adam told me.'

'Do you feel angry with him?'

'Very angry,' she said. 'But also very sad. I feel sorry for anyone who gets into such a mess.'

'Where does it leave you, Bella?' Mark asked kindly.

'Up to my neck in it. Dealing with Adam on his own was difficult enough. Now I've got involved with his family.' She shivered. 'Not to mention Jez.'

'Who's he?'

'Some jerk from the disco. He's frightening. Jez jumped on me as I was leaving the hospital yesterday. He claims that Adam owes him money. Jez told me to pass a message on — Adam's got to pay up or else.' Another shiver ran through her. 'It was horrible, Mark. What should I do?'

'Report him to security,' said Mark, putting a protective hand on her arm. 'They won't let someone like that hang around the hospital. To make sure he doesn't bother you again, take simple precautions. Stay in a group at all times. I'll go to and from the hospital with you.'

'Thanks, Mark. You're a real friend.'

'This is not your fight, Bella. Pull out.'

'If only I could. It's getting so complicated. I just hope Sarah may be able to sort it all out.'

'Sarah?'

'Adam's ex-girlfriend. Mr Green seemed to think she was the one person who could get Adam back on the right track. I'm going to find her.'

'Why doesn't Mr Green try and find her himself?'

'He's lost touch with her. Also, I think he's embarrassed. It's not easy telling someone your son's become an addict. Mr Green's bound to feel responsible. If I can find Sarah, I can put her in the picture.'

'Give me a shout if you need any help.'

'Thanks, Mark.'

'I'll go with you if you don't want to meet this Sarah on your own.'

Bella was touched. 'Would you do that for me?'

'Just say the word.'

'I will, Mark.' She sipped her orange juice. 'I owe you a great big favour for this.'

'As it happens, I could use a spot of advice.'

'Ask away.'

'Imagine you're out on a first date with a bloke you like.'

'Story of my life!'

'You're wearing a beautiful white silk shirt...'

She laughed. 'Nothing else?'

'And he accidentally spills his beer over it. What would you do?'

'Throttle him.'

Mark wished he'd never asked.

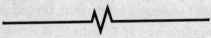

Karlene was very surprised to see her there. Virginia Tyc was not due back at the hospital for another week. Yet she was the first person through the door that morning. She looked even more harassed than ever. Karlene saw Catherine White, the senior physiotherapist, take the patient into her office for a private consultation. When Mrs Tyc finally emerged, she seemed a little reassured.

Karlene crossed the room towards her.

'Good morning, Mrs Tyc.'

'Oh — hello.'

'Problems?' enquired Karlene.

'I had a pain in my arm last night. It kept me awake.'

'I'm sorry to hear that.'

'Mrs White explained that it was quite normal,' said the woman. 'There's nothing wrong. The bones have knitted together properly — the X-ray showed that. But she said there's bound to be a little discomfort when the plaster first comes off.'

'Yes,' said Karlene. 'That happened to me when

I broke my ankle at school. For weeks after they took the cast off, I had a dull ache. It made me afraid to put my full weight on the ankle.'

'Mrs White's given me some exercises to do. And I've got some painkillers from my doctor. Mrs White warned me not to overdo it. But I don't have any choice.' She became agitated. 'I've got a husband and two children to look after. A house to clean and a part-time job in the evenings. I get no time to put my feet up.'

'Where do you work, Mrs Tyc?'

'In a launderette.'

'Doesn't that involve a lot of lifting? A basket of clothes must be quite heavy.'

'It was a bit of a struggle when I had the plaster on.'

Karlene was shocked. 'Didn't you give up work?'

'My husband wouldn't like it.'

'But your arm should have been in a sling at first,' said Karlene.

'It was — most of the time,' said Virginia Tyc with a hopeless shrug. 'But I couldn't afford to. We need the money.'

Karlene felt even more sympathy for her. Her make-up had been less careful that morning and the bruise was more obvious. Karlene had only met her twice but she could feel her distress. She suspected that Mrs Tyc had lots of other bruises —

on the inside.

'I have to go,' she said.

'One last thing...' Karlene tried to speak.

'Sorry, I can't stay. My husband's waiting for me.'

Before Karlene could ask about her facial injury, the woman turned on her heel and hurried away. She was plainly terrified of keeping her husband waiting any longer. Karlene's curiosity was aroused. She went to the window and watched until the couple came out of the building.

What she saw, made her stare in astonishment; Karlene had imagined Mr Tyc would be a big, brawny man with an intimidating manner. In fact, he was short and slight. He wore overalls and a cap. Instead of being angry with his wife, he had his arm around her as they walked towards the main gate.

Karlene felt suddenly guilty for judging the man so harshly. She'd obviously been completely wrong about him.

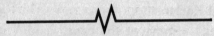

Suzie went to Rainbow Ward during Visiting Time. She was shown to the sideward by a nurse who went in alone and came out with Olwyn French, a plump woman with a florid complexion. Mrs French was puzzled by a stranger visiting her daughter. Suzie introduced herself.

'Hello, Mrs French,' she said. 'Sorry to disturb

you. My name's Suzie Hembrow. I'm a trainee radiographer here. I met your son a couple of times.'

'Tim?'

'That's right.'

'Not caused any trouble, has he?' asked Olwyn French. 'He's a bit of a scamp. What's he done this time?'

'Nothing,' said Suzie. 'But he was telling me about his sister, Donna. I just looked in to see how she was.'

The woman's manner changed at once. Her anxious frown was replaced by a warm smile. She dismissed the nurse with a nod then stood aside to let Suzie through.

'That's very kind of you,' she said. 'Come in and see her for yourself.'

'I don't want to intrude.'

'Donna likes meeting new people. In you come.'

Suzie went into the room with some trepidation. Tim had mentioned a machine and Suzie had feared it would be a life-support machine. She thought his sister might be lying in a coma.

But Donna French was sitting in a chair and was connected by a tube to a different type of machine altogether. Suzie recognised it from some photographs she'd seen in her medical textbook. It was a dialysis machine. The poor girl evidently had a problem with her kidneys.

'This is Suzie,' said the mother. 'Say hello, Donna.'

'Hello.'

'How are you?' asked Suzie.

'I don't like it in here.'

'It won't be for long,' soothed Mrs French. 'They've got to make you better. That's why you're in hospital.'

'I still don't like it, Mum.'

Donna was a thin girl with straggly hair and a brace on her teeth. She bore a strong resemblance to her brother. Both of them had an air of mischief about them, though it was more subdued in Donna's case. Being so ill had taken the edge off her cheeky spirit.

'I know your brother,' said Suzie. The girl brightened. 'We keep bumping into each other.'

'Tim's great. He's been every day so far.'

'Yes,' said her mother with a grin. 'Young devil has sneaked off school to visit Donna. Any excuse to miss work.'

'I see he's a Manchester United supporter,' said Suzie.

'He watches football on telly,' said Donna. 'I support them, too. I like watching Top of the Pops and Neighbours, too. They've got a telly here but I can't get to it.'

'You can watch all the telly you like when you're better,' said her mother, indulgently, stroking her daughter's hair.

'Can I choose the programmes?'

'Yes, love.'

'You won't let Tim choose, will you?'

'You can watch whatever you like.'

Olwyn French was warm and motherly. It was clear from all the bags she'd brought with her that she would be there for most of the day. She might even stay the night so that she could be a constant support to Donna.

Suzie chatted happily with them for a few minutes then started to say goodbye. As she was going, she threw in a casual question.

'Does Tim have a white rabbit, by any chance?'

'He doesn't,' said Mrs French, 'but Donna does.'

Suzie caught the girl's eye and saw the fearful look in it. Donna was afraid she'd been found out. She knew pets weren't allowed inside the hospital. If Tim was caught smuggling in the rabbit, he'd be reported. Suzie winked at her to let her know that her secret was safe. A wonderful smile broke out on Donna's face.

'His name's Bobo,' she said.

'I'll remember that,' said Suzie.

'Will you come again?' asked Donna, eagerly.

'Yes, Donna. Whenever I get the chance.'

Olwyn French showed Suzie out of the side ward and thanked her for coming. Suzie glanced back at the girl.

'How long is Donna likely to be in here?'

'Until they find a donor. She's very poorly.

Donna will only pull through if she has a kidney transplant.'

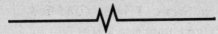

Bella had a frustrating time in the hospital telephone booth. The only information she had about Sarah Baker was that the girl had once lived on Mount Pleasant Estate. Bella assumed she could simply look up the surname in the directory and get straight through to Sarah's family. She hadn't realised how big an estate Mount Pleasant was. There were eleven Bakers listed for that area alone.

Bella worked her way through eight of them before she finally dialled the right number. When the receiver was picked up, she heard a woman's voice.

'5378446,' she said.

'Oh, hello,' said Bella. 'Mrs Baker?'

'Yes.'

'Does a Sarah Baker live there, by any chance?'

There was a pause. 'She did... yes.'

'Thank goodness!'

'Who is this, please?'

'You don't know me, Mrs Baker. My name is Bella Denton.'

'What do you want?' asked the woman, guardedly.

'I'm a friend of Adam Green.'

'Then I've nothing to say to you.'

'Please, don't ring off,' pleaded Bella. 'You've no idea how long it's taken me to find you. I need to speak to Sarah. I just wondered if you could possibly give me her address?'

Bella heard a gasp and then there was another long pause.

'Leave us alone,' hissed the voice.

'Is it so much to ask?'

'It's very cruel of you to ring up like this.'

'Just tell me where I can reach Sarah, please.'

'Is this some kind of joke?'

'What do you mean?'

'I can't give you Sarah's address,' said the woman, angry now. 'Adam should know that. My daughter died over a month ago.'

She slammed down the receiver. Bella gazed at the phone in her hand, stunned.

CHAPTER NINE

'How serious is the case?' asked Damian Holt.

'Very serious,' said Suzie. 'The girl is on a dialysis machine. She needs a kidney transplant.'

'Sounds like renal failure to me.'

'What exactly is that, Damian?'

'I haven't got time to go into too much detail,' he said, 'so you'll have to make do with a short answer. The kidneys are a vital part of the urinary tract. We all have two. Their job is to filter all the waste substances out of the blood to keep it purified. The kidneys consist of millions of filtering units which are supplied with blood from the renal artery.'

Suzie listened with interest. She'd had a chance encounter with Damian in a corridor at the hospital, and had taken advantage of it. The handsome young Australian doctor was one of Bella's ex-boyfriends. Suzie had always found him very friendly.

He flashed a grin. 'Does any of that help?'

'Yes, Damian. But tell me about transplants.'

'Kidneys are top of the league,' he explained. 'There are seven or eight times as many kidney transplants done as heart transplants.'

'Is that because it's an easier operation?'

'Partly. Though transplant surgery's always difficult. The advantage of a kidney is that it can be kept viable for twenty-four hours in cold storage. A heart has to be removed and implanted within three hours.'

'What are Donna's chances, do you think?'

'I can't comment on that, Suzie. I don't know the details of this particular case.'

'Assuming a donor is found, is the operation straightforward?'

'No, it's complex. The main problem for this girl is not surgical,' he said. 'It's finding a donor in the first place. There are patients all over the country waiting for kidneys — the trouble is the demand will always be greater than the supply.'

Suzie thanked him for his help and apologised for holding him up. She'd only ever met him at social events before. Now she'd seen him on duty, she was very impressed. He was pleasant and well-informed.

'How's Bella?' he asked.

'Fine.'

'Say hi to her for me, won't you?'

'Of course.'

'Haven't seen her around for a while.'

'Oh, Bella's still here,' said Suzie with a smile. 'This hospital wouldn't be quite the same place without her.'

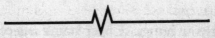

Louise Webb was studying a textbook with great concentration. At first, she didn't see him. Mark was able to watch her quietly for several minutes. He noted the title of her book — 'Care of Patients With Psychiatric Problems.'

Then she glanced up from the table. Her eyes crinkled into a half-smile but there was no excitement in her manner.

Mark crossed his fingers and plunged straight in.

'I was just wondering, Louise... There's an end-of-term dance coming up.'

'It's nearly six weeks away.'

'I like to plan well in advance,' he said. 'I suppose you'll be going.'

'Probably.'

'Shall I get two tickets, then?'

Louise hesitated. She wasn't sure if she wanted to accept Mark's invitation but she didn't want to hurt his feelings. She found a compromise.

'Ask me nearer the time,' she suggested.

'But someone else might get in before me.'

'No, they won't,' she promised. 'I'm not up for grabs. I just need a breathing space, that's all. Ask me in a month.'

Mark was content. He felt he'd made some more progress. Louise hadn't rejected him. He was storing up her goodwill. With his next breath, he threw it away.

'Did you get those beer stains out of your silk shirt?' he asked.

'No,' she said. 'It's ruined.'

So saying, she picked up her book. The chat was over.

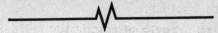

Bella was hoping for a chance to speak to Philip Green again. She was still shocked about what she'd heard about Sarah Baker and wanted to pass it on to him. But when she walked into Reception to look for him. it was his wife she saw.

Judith Green was sitting on her own, leafing through a copy of *Ideal Home*. She looked more serene than on the previous occasion. When Bella went over to her, she looked up with a polite smile and put the magazine aside.

'Hello,' she said.

'Is your husband here this evening?' asked Bella.

'Yes, he's visiting Adam.'

'Are you going to see him as well?'

'What use would that be? We only seem to irritate each other. Besides, Philip wouldn't let me.'

'Why not?'

'According to him, Adam's very changeable.'

'He is!' said Bella with feeling.

'I wouldn't want to set him off again.'

Bella warmed to her slightly. The supercilious manner had gone. Judith Green was doing her best to remain calm.

'I think I owe you an apology, Bella — for some of the things I said to you the other night.'

'They were a bit unfair, Mrs Green.'

'I was objectionable. Philip was very cross with me.'

'It was a difficult situation.'

'Only one of many, believe me!'

Bella studied her for a moment - she wondered why Mrs Green got on so badly with her stepson. There must have been a time when relations between them were happier.

'Do you have any children of your own?' she asked.

'No, my first husband didn't want a family, so eventually, I gave up wanting one, too.'

'You've got a son, now,' Bella pointed out.

'Yes,' said Judith, wistfully. 'The idea really appealed to me when Philip asked me to marry him. I had no experience of being a mother — especially to a teenage son — but I was willing to learn.' She shook her head. 'Unfortunately, Adam was less willing to learn. He just shut me out — for all sorts of reasons I suppose. Starting with the obvious one.'

'You're not his real mother?' suggested Bella.

'And never can be. He still misses her dreadfully,' said Mrs Green.

'What happened to her?'

'She died of leukaemia when he was only ten.'

Bella felt very sympathetic towards Adam. She knew from personal experience how hard that could be. She'd lost her own father after a long and painful illness. In Adam's mind, nobody could ever take the place of his real mother. Mrs Green was an intruder to him.

'My husband's tried so hard with him. Philip's bent over backwards to help Adam. But he gets no thanks. The more you do for him, the less respect he has for you.' A flash of temper ignited her eyes. 'That's what makes me mad. The disrespect. I mean, we give him a house and a home — he owes us some recognition.'

'Was he always this way?'

'Not when Sarah was around. After she left, he flipped.'

Bella bit back her rejoinder. She didn't want to say anything about Sarah's death until she'd spoken to Mr Green.

There was a long pause. Now Judith was calm again.

'It was the pendant,' she murmured. 'My opal pendant. It was a wedding present from my husband. It was the most beautiful piece of jewellery I'd ever had.'

'What happened to it?'

'Adam took it.'

'You mean he stole your pendant?'

'He knew just how much it would hurt me. First of all, he took money to buy drugs, then he took things he could sell for money; then the pendant.'

'What did he do with it?'

'He wouldn't say. I'd have offered him any amount of money to get it back but Adam wouldn't tell me where it was. I'll never forgive him for that.'

'Did you report him to the police?'

'Philip wouldn't hear of it,' said the woman, bitterly. 'He felt that we should "contain" the problem. Look at the result — Adam collapses again and is rushed back here.'

She took out her handkerchief and sobbed quietly into it. Bella felt terrible. She put a comforting arm on Mrs Green's shoulder. The story about the pendant gave her some insight into why she resented her stepson so much. It also changed Bella's feelings towards Adam. She was even more wary of him now.

Philip Green came striding towards them. Bella was keen to talk to him but he was in no mood for conversation. His face looked flushed and his jaw tight. He took his wife by the arm and helped her up from the chair.

'Come on, Judith,' he said. 'We're getting out of here.'

'Could I have a moment, please?' said Bella.

'Not now, Bella.'

'But it's very important,' insisted Bella.

'Ring me later. I'm in the book.'

'Have you seen Adam?'

'I'll tell you about that when I've calmed down a little,' he said, moving away. 'Even my patience ran

92

out this evening.'

'Would they let me see Adam now?'

'Stay away from him, Bella. It's not a good time.'

He hustled his wife across Reception and out through the main door. Bella was bewildered by the Green family. This time, the haughty wife had been pleasant and reasonable and the quiet father had been in a rage. What was going on?

It was time to go. Mark was waiting in the college of nurses to escort her home. But as she came out into the car park, someone else was waiting to see her. Jez lurched out from behind a parked van.

'Did you deliver my message?' he snarled.

'No!' she cried.

'I want my money!'

'It's nothing to do with me.'

'Go back in there and get it!'

'Leave me alone!' she screamed.

'Go back!' Jez ordered, grabbing her arm. 'Tell Adam to pay up or I'll come after him myself.'

'You're hurting me,' she said, struggling to get away.

'Do as I tell you!'

Bella wanted to shout for help but the sight of Jez took all her breath away. His mouth was set in a manic grin. His eyes looked wild and his strong fingers dug into her flesh.

'Hey! What are you doing!' yelled a voice.

Running footsteps made them turn. A figure was

charging across the car park towards them. It was Gordy.

'Let go of her!' he shouted.

Jez was bigger than Gordy but not ready for a fight. The noise would alert the security guards. Jez brought his face right up to Bella's then lurched off towards the exit. She was shaking with fear by now.

'Who the hell was that?' said Gordy, coming up to her.

Bella flung herself gratefully into his arms.

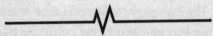

Suzie finished later than usual at the hospital. As she came down the stairs, she considered dropping in to see Donna French again. The girl's condition saddened her. Renal failure was terrible at any age but it seemed particularly cruel in a child. Donna might have a very long wait for a donor. It would be difficult to keep up her spirits.

'Hello.'

Suzie heard the voice but couldn't see who was speaking.

'I'm over here.'

She recognised Tim's voice this time but she still had no idea where he was. Then she saw a skinny hand poking round the edge of a door. The index finger was crooked.

Suzie crossed over to what she discovered was a little storeroom. Tim's head came round the door.

'What on earth are you doing in here, Tim?'

'Waiting till they go — the nurses on Donna's ward. They take their break soon. That's when I can get in to see her.'

'But you're her brother,' said Suzie. 'You can visit her more or less any time.'

'I can,' he said, smiling cheekily, 'but Bobo can't.'

Suzie smiled. 'I knew it had to be your rabbit.'

'It's Donna's. She looks after him at home.'

'Strictly speaking, Bobo shouldn't be here.'

'You won't tell on us, will you?'

'Well...'

'Donna said you was a friend. Friends don't tell.'

'Pets just aren't allowed, Tim,' she said, feeling that he should understand why. 'Think what it would be like if every child in here had their pet rabbit or cat or dog. It would be chaos. And there's the problem of hygiene.'

'Bobo's dead clean,' he said.

'I'm sure he is,' said Suzie.

Tim's face seemed to crumple with fear. 'Will she be all right?'

'Donna? I hope so, Tim.'

'They keep saying she's got to have this operation but they won't tell me what it is. Something about a donor.'

'That's right. Your sister has a problem with her kidneys. She needs a transplant. That means she has to get a healthy kidney from someone else. It's an operation they've done here many times. If it's successful — and I'm sure it will be in Donna's case — she'll be able to leave hospital in time.'

'I hope so,' he said. 'I really miss her. So does Bobo.' He became defensive. 'Don't tell on us, will you?'

He searched her face for reassurance in the same way that his sister had. Suzie smiled again and shook her head.

'I won't say anything,' she promised. 'As long as you don't make a habit of it. Is that fair?'

'Yeah.' He lowered his voice. 'Wanna see him?'

He pulled Suzie into the storeroom and shut the door. Tim was wearing a loose fitting anorak over his sweatshirt. A faint odour told her that the rabbit was also in there but she couldn't actually see it. There was no sports bag this time.

The boy's grin went from ear to ear.

'D'you know where he is?'

'I haven't a clue, Tim. You brought him in a carrier bag the first time.'

'He got out of that,' said Tim. 'And the man at the gate gave me a funny look when I brought him in my sports bag. He asked me what I was carrying.'

'So how did you get past security this evening?'

'Like this.'

Tim pulled the anorak open to reveal a large pouch that had been sewn into it. Bella could see the animal squirming around. Dipping a hand into the pouch, the boy pulled out the white rabbit and held him up to the light.

'Here he is,' he said, proudly.

The rabbit blinked at Suzie.

'Hello, Bobo,' she said. 'Nice to meet you properly at last.'

Bella had never been so glad to see him — Gordy had come to her rescue at precisely the right time. When they'd collected Mark, they went off to the wine bar nearby. Bella felt she needed a restorative drink.

'Jez is horrible,' she said. 'He terrifies me.'

'I should have been there,' said Mark, annoyed with himself for not guarding her more carefully. 'Why didn't you tell me you were going across to the hospital?'

'He's gone now,' said Gordy, 'that's the main thing. I'll make sure security get a description of him. We don't want him loitering around there again.'

'Jez won't give up that easily,' said Bella.

'We'll be ready for him,' promised Mark.

'Who exactly is he?' asked Gordy.

'I've no idea,' she said with a shiver of apprehension. 'Jez showed up at *Underworld* that night and had a row with Adam. Then he rolled up here, asking for money that he reckons is owed to him.'

'Is Jez a supplier? Does he sell drugs to Adam?'

'I don't know, Mark,' she said. 'But I'm certain of one thing. Jez is on something himself. I've looked right into those hideous eyes of his. He gives me the creeps.'

Gordy gave her time to recover from the shock of the encounter and then he reminded her of his advice at the start.

'You should've stayed well out of it, Bel.'

'I know that now.'

'Adam Green had "trouble" written all over him.'

'Don't rub it in.'

'Remember what Sister Killeen always says,' reminded Mark. 'Never get involved with the patients. It's fatal.'

'But he wasn't a patient when I met him,' she protested. 'He was just a cool guy at a disco who asked me to dance. I didn't realize all this would happen.'

'Neither did I,' said Gordy. 'And I'm sorry for leaving you to cope on your own. From now on, I'm in this as well.'

'So am I, Bella,' added Mark. 'You can count on us.'

'I will — don't worry!'

'Did you manage to track down Sarah?'

Bella nodded sadly. 'I'm afraid I did. Sarah's not in a position to see anybody, Mark. She died over a month ago.'

Mark and Gordy were stunned. Bella told them about her brief telephone conversation with the girl's mother.

'Did she happen to mention the cause of death?' asked Gordy.

'No,' said Bella. 'She was too deeply upset. I could hear it in her voice. It made me feel guilty, bothering her like that. I mean, Sarah could only have been *our* age.'

'Does Adam know about this?' asked Mark.

'I'm not sure.'

'Well, it's not your job to tell him,' warned Gordy. 'He had a funny turn when you mentioned her name. If you tell him that Sarah's actually dead — and he hasn't heard already — there's no knowing what Adam might do.'

'I tried to tell his father so that he could tell Adam,' said Bella. 'But he charged out of the hospital before I could even speak to him. That's when I bumped into Jez.'

'Poor old Bel!' he said. 'One way and another, you've had a pretty lousy day. And all because of Adam Green and his family. Maybe you should tell them all to get lost.'

It was a tempting idea but she was now so involved that it would be difficult to break free. She was angry with Adam for deceiving her but that only made her want to confront him and not run away. She felt sorry for his father and even had some sympathy for his stepmother now. And the news about Sarah had shaken her; it had also made her even more curious about exactly what had happened between her and Adam. She also wanted to find out how Jez fitted into the story.

They finished their drinks and Mark got to his feet.

'Another round?' he said.

'A quick one, then,' said Bella.

Gordy drained his glass. 'Thanks, Marco.'

Mark had only six paces to walk to the bar but they proved beyond him. As he tried to walk, his head began to spin and he pitched forward. He grabbed at an empty table to steady himself.

'Are you OK?' said Bella in alarm.

'Fine, fine,' he said, straightening up. 'I slipped.'

'You mean, there really *was* a white rabbit?' asked Karlene.

'His name's Bobo.'

'You've actually seen him?'

'Yes,' said Suzie. 'Seen him, held him and stroked his fur. He's wonderful.'

'He's also quite illegal. Any live animal is a health risk as well as a hazard. Bobo may be wonderful but he's got no place inside a hospital.'

'I did tell Tim that.'

'Did he accept it, though?'

'Eventually,' said Suzie. 'I couldn't be too hard on the poor kid. He'd gone to such lengths to get his sister's pet in to cheer her up. Donna was over the moon about it.'

Karlene grinned. 'At least it's only a rabbit.

Suppose she'd got a St Bernard?'

'Tim would've found a way to smuggle that in as well,' said Suzie, grinning.

'That kid will go far.'

They were strolling across the car park together at the end of the day. Karlene was pleased that the white rabbit had finally been identified — it would silence Gordy's endless teasing. Like Suzie, her real sympathy lay with Donna French.

'What an awful situation to be in!' she said.

'Just seven years old and tied to a dialysis machine.'

'I wonder how long she'll have to wait for a donor? And even if one is found, her problems aren't over.'

'No,' said Suzie with a sigh. 'According to Damian Holt, kidney transplants are by no means routine operations. Some very complicated surgery is involved.'

Karlene shook herself. 'We are a gloomy pair! Fearing the worst. We ought to look on the bright side, Suzie. The little girl is in the best possible place. This hospital has an excellent record for transplant surgery. It may all turn out fine.'

'I'm sure it will. If only a donor can be found. I'm keeping my fingers well and truly crossed for Donna.'

'What about Bobo?'

'I'll hold my fingers to my nose when he's

around,' she joked.

They were laughing as they came round the angle of the hospital. Facing them was the Casualty Department. Paramedics were lifting a patient out of the rear of an ambulance on a stretcher. Karlene looked casually in their direction.

But when a taxi pulled up at the kerb, to let a woman jump out, she looked more curious. With one hand wrapped in a towel, the passenger used the other one to thrust some money at the driver before walking slowly into Casualty. Karlene stared.

'Someone you know?' asked Suzie.

'I think so — I think it was Mrs Tyc.'

'Is she the one with the Polish husband?'

'That's her — she was in again today. Now it looks as if she's back for a third time.'

'Why not go and find out?'

'Do you mind?'

'Of course not,' said Suzie. 'I don't know if it was Mrs Tyc or not, but the woman who got out of that taxi was in a state. Shall I wait while you run in?'

'No,' said Karlene. 'I'd bet anything it was her. I know that apologetic shuffle of hers. You go on home, Suzie. I could be here for some time.'

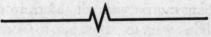

Bella felt less tense after her drink and heartened by the presence of her two friends. By the time she left the wine bar, the brush with Jez was no more than a distant memory. With Gordy and Mark either side of her, she felt very safe. Bella linked arms with them as she strode along.

'Who shall I take to the end-of-term dance?' she said.

Gordy laughed. 'The idea is that some guy takes *you*.'

'How old-fashioned! I prefer to do the asking. That way you stand a better chance of getting who you want.'

'And who do you want?' asked Mark.

'Someone cute, with a nice bottom and a sense of humour.'

'In that case, you'd better take me,' volunteered Gordy.

'It's not for ages yet,' said Bella, airily. 'I've got plenty of time to audition people. Let me see now — if I get through two a week...'

'Only two,' teased Gordy. 'You're slipping, Bel... What about you, Marco? Who are you taking?'

'I don't know yet,' said Mark.

'Who would you like to take?'

'Wait and see.'

'You're a dark horse, aren't you?'

Bella knew quite well who Mark would choose but she didn't want to expose him to Gordy's taunts. Things were obviously not going well between Mark and Louise. He would be very sensitive to any teasing on that subject.

As she looked up, she saw their house in the distance.

'Home sweet home!' she said, sincerely.

'Somebody's waiting for us,' noted Mark.

Bella was suddenly alert. 'It's not Jez, is it? I couldn't face him again.'

'It's Mrs Jeffries, she's holding something.'

As they got closer, they saw that it was Enid Jeffries. She was the old woman who lived next door to them. She was carrying a bunch of flowers wrapped in tissue paper. As Bella came up, she handed them over to her. The dozen red roses had an amazing scent.

Bella was overwhelmed. 'For me?' she asked.

'Yes,' said Mrs Jeffries. 'They came half-an-hour ago. From the hospital.'

'The hospital?' echoed Gordy. 'You're supposed to take flowers in there not send them out.'

'They were brought by one of the porters,' explained the old woman. 'He did give me his name — a short man with shiny hair and a centre parting.'

'Mick Morris?' said Mark.

'That's right.'

'Everybody knows Mick. He runs errands.'

'Go on, Bel,' urged Gordy. 'Put us out of our misery. Find out who sent them.'

She took out the card and read the scribbled message.

'Oh no!' she said. 'They're from Adam Green.'

It was a long wait for Karlene. When she walked into Casualty there was no sign of Virginia Tyc. That suggested her wound was serious. Several other patients were waiting for attention to minor injuries. If Mrs Tyc had jumped the queue, there had to be a good medical reason. It made Karlene even more determined to sit it out.

When Mrs Tyc finally appeared, she was brought out by a nurse who guided her to a chair. Her left hand was heavily bandaged and in a sling. She looked very distressed. As the nurse went back to her duties, Karlene walked across to see her.

'Hello, Mrs Tyc,' she said.

'Oh...hello.'

'What are you doing here?'

'I've hurt my hand, slicing some tomatoes,' she said. 'My own fault.'

'Did you have to have stitches?'

'Fourteen. They gave me an injection as well.'

'Tetanus, probably.'

Virginia Tyc looked down at her hand in alarm.

'It's throbbing,' she said. 'And I lost a lot of blood.'

'Why didn't your husband bring you to the hospital?'

'He had to look after the children.'

'Did he know how bad the injury was?' asked Karlene.

Mrs Tyc shook her head. She seemed dazed and Karlene didn't believe her story for a moment. Slicing tomatoes might cause a nasty gash but it was unlikely she'd need fourteen stitches. The wound was probably done in some other way.

'The doctor told me to wait until I felt ready to go,' she explained. 'They're going to send me home in an ambulance.'

'In that case, you could go straightaway.'

'No.' She was adamant. 'I'm staying here for a bit.'

'Won't your husband be worried about you?'

Karlene saw the woman's lips begin to tremble. Old suspicions came back.

'Can you manage on your own?' she said, gently.

'I'll just have to.'

'I could help you, Mrs Tyc. You're obviously very shaken. Couldn't you use a bit of assistance?'

'I can manage, thank you.'

'Not with your hand bound up like that. You won't be able to cook — or put the children to bed. Why not let me help out? It's no bother, honestly.'

'I'll get by somehow. I always do.'

The resignation in her voice was quite pitiful. It made Karlene even more sympathetic. She suspected the injury was no kitchen accident but it wasn't her place to pry into the poor woman's private life.

Virginia Tyc looked at her with a mixture of curiosity and fear. She found Karlene's offer of help very touching but she was clearly afraid to accept it.

'You're very kind,' she said.

'Call on me any time.'

'My husband wouldn't like that.'

'It's not up to him, surely?' said Karlene. 'You're the one who needs the help, Mrs Tyc. Not him.'

'He hates having strangers in the house.'

'I'd be there as your friend.'

'It wouldn't work, I'm afraid.'

Virginia Tyc fell silent. She stared ahead of her, her eyes glazed, as she remembered what had happened. She felt the knife going into her flesh again; the pain was searing. She let out a cry of anguish.

Karlene leant towards her, putting an arm around her, comfortingly.

'You're in no fit state to do all the chores, Mrs Tyc. Why not let someone else take the strain? I'd love to help out.'

'Leave me alone!' she yelled, suddenly angry. 'This is none of your business. I cut my hand and that's all there is to it. I'll manage. Now go away. I want to go home!'

Bella was in a quandary. Common sense told her to keep away from Adam Green but the flowers had touched her. It was his way of expressing thanks. He was confused and needed help. She didn't want to let him down.

Mark and Gordy tried to warn her again.

'Don't go back there,' said Mark.

'You'd be crazy!' said Gordy.

Bella looked at the red roses, now standing in a vase.

'Adam has a lot of problems,' she said, 'but he still found time to think of me. I'm going to visit him now.'

Gordy waved his arms. 'I won't let you, Bel!'

'Remember what his father said,' observed Mark. 'It's not a good time to see Adam. You told us that even Mr Green lost his patience with him.'

'Adam will have calmed down by now,' she said. 'He sent those flowers. That's not the kind of thing you do in a temper. It's a message — Adam is anxious to see me. He wants to change and the flowers are a sign of that.'

Gordy was blunt. 'All he wants to do is get you back there, Bel. He's obsessed with you. Can't you see that? He'll use you. How many danger signals do you need?'

'I'm going,' she said, firmly. 'And that's that.'

Unable to dissuade her, the two friends insisted on going with her to the hospital. They took her all the way to the door of the recreation room but Bella went in alone.

'Hello, Adam,' she said.

'Bella!'

'How are you?'

'I'm fine.'

'That's not what your father told me. I met him as he was leaving the hospital.'

'Oh, yes,' he said, dismissively. 'We had a bit of a row, that's all. Nothing serious. Dad went off in a huff.'

Adam was watching television when she came in. He looked fit and relaxed. It was difficult to believe there was anything wrong with him. He was delighted to see her and reached out to take her hands. Bella drew back slightly — she was very much on guard.

'Did you get my flowers?' he asked.

'Thanks — they were beautiful.'

'I hoped they'd bring you back.'

Bella was watching him carefully. He seemed calm enough but she knew how quickly his mood could change. And she also remembered how many lies he'd told her in the short time she'd known him. Adam couldn't be trusted.

'What was the row about?' she said.

'Oh, that. Usual thing. Judith. Dad wants me to make more of an effort to be nice to her. It's his condition for having me back in the house. I told him it was time she started being nice to *me*.'

'Then what?'

'He stormed out.'

Bella suspected there was more to it than that. Philip Green seemed a tolerant man; he would need to be pushed to the limit before he exploded. Bella put the matter aside. Adam's father was no threat to her. But someone else was.

'I met that awful Jez,' she said, quietly. 'He was hanging around in Reception.'

Adam was alarmed. 'Jez is *here*? What did he want?'

'To get a message to you.'

'I can guess what that is,' said Adam, hotly.

'He tried to bully me into delivering it — but I refused. I'm not playing postman for a creep like that.'

'You don't need to, Bella,' he said. 'I know what he wants. Jez claims I owe him money — but it's not true. I've paid him. I settled that debt ages ago.'

'So you did borrow money from him?'

'Not money. Jez loaned me something else.'

'He's determined to get it back.'

'Tough!'

'Adam, he's leapt on me twice now,' she said, hotly. 'He frightened the daylights out of me. I think

I'm entitled to know what's going on. He's dangerous.'

'Yeah, Jez can be,' he admitted.

'I don't want him near me.'

'He shouldn't have bothered you, Bella. It won't happen again. He's a creep. Forget him.'

'How can I when he keeps jumping out at me. Who *is* he?'

Adam took a deep breath. He could see Bella was upset. She deserved some kind of explanation. He weighed his words carefully because he didn't want to frighten her away.

'Jez and I go back a long way,' he said.

'So he *is* a friend?' said Bella.

'Not really. We were at school together. He was always a bit of a thug. I kept out of his way — so did Sarah.'

'Sarah Baker, you mean?'

'Jez fancied her, kept asking her out.'

'But he's revolting.'

'That didn't put him off,' said Adam. 'Sarah couldn't stand him. She turned to me to protect her. Jez Halliday was as jealous as hell. He's never forgiven me for that. He claimed I'd taken Sarah away from me. It wasn't like that. She hated him.'

'So why did you stay in touch?'

'I didn't, Bella. It was Jez who found me.'

'On the drug scene? Come on Adam, tell me the truth.'

'I have. That night at *Underworld* was my first time.'

'Not according to your father,' she said. 'He told me you'd had a drug problem for six months at least. This is the second time you've been admitted to hospital.' A long pause. 'Well — isn't it?'

A pained look came into his eyes. He shifted uneasily.

'That was never my real world, Bella,' he said. 'I never sank as low as Jez and his mates. He's into hard drugs. You know — heroin, cocaine. Jez is an addict. Not me — all I've ever touched is the harmless stuff. Cannabis and Ecstasy.'

'But it's not harmless or you wouldn't be in here.'

'I was stupid — mixed the pills up.'

'You still haven't told me what you had from Jez.'

'Some acid, that's all. I met him in a pub one night when I was feeling depressed.'

Bella was shocked. 'You took LSD?'

'It's not addictive,' he said, defensively. 'Besides, I had a bad trip. It screwed me up. Put me off acid for good. And I did pay Jez. I remember clearly. I gave him his money.'

'So why is he still after you for it?'

'Because that's the kind of guy he is.'

'You're hiding something from me, Adam.'

'Of course I'm not.'

'I can't help you if you lie to me.'

'I've been honest with you, Bella.'

'I'm sure there's something you're not telling me.'

Suddenly, Adam erupted with rage. 'Look — get off my back, will you?' he yelled. 'Questions, questions, questions! You're worse than the doctors here. They never believe me either. I thought you were different from them, Bella.'

'I'm on your side, remember.'

'Get out!' he shouted, losing control completely. 'Who asked you to come here, anyway? It's my life. Stop trying to run it for me! Get out, will you! Go on — out!'

Bella backed away in alarm. He was going crazy.

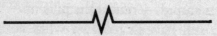

Karlene lay back in the armchair and shook her head.

'Something about that woman worries me,' she said.

'What is it?' asked Suzie.

'That's the trouble. I'm not sure. It's almost as if Mrs Tyc *wants* my help but is afraid to ask.'

'I thought she told you to leave her alone.'

'That was just a defence, Suzie.'

'Suppose she really *did* cut her hand on a kitchen knife?'

'Somebody else might've been holding the knife.'

Suzie was startled. She looked up from the newspaper.

'Are you accusing her husband?' she said.

'It's a possibility.'

'But I thought you actually saw her husband, Karlene. You said he looked quite harmless.'

'So did Dr Crippen.'

'So why is he suddenly a prime suspect again?'

'Because of the way she behaved in Casualty.'

'Do you think he attacked her with a knife?'

'I don't know, Suzie,' she said. 'I just have this gut feeling that she lives in terror of her husband. OK, he seemed no threat at all when I saw him at the hospital. But he might have been on his best behaviour, then.'

'It's still a very serious charge.'

'Yes, and it's a pity that we'll never know the truth. Mrs Tyc will run a mile whenever she sees me now. She knows I suspect the truth. I've seen the symptoms before,' continued Karlene, earnestly. 'There was a woman who lived in our street. She had the same apologetic walk, the same don't-hit-me look on her face. Her husband was a quiet little man, who wouldn't say boo to a goose. He was the last person you'd expect of wife-battering.'

'And is that what he did?'

'Yes, Suzie — behind closed doors. It went on for years before we found out. All because we didn't pick up the signals. What that poor woman must have gone through! I hate to think of Mrs Tyc being in the same boat.'

'When is she due back with the physios?'

'Not until next week. And I won't be observing in that department then.' She shrugged. 'It'll be too late.'

The doorbell rang. Suzie went to see who it was. Seconds later, she returned with a short, neat man with his hair in a centre parting. It was Mick Morris, the hospital porter. They both knew him by sight.

Their visitor seemed extremely embarrassed.

'I'd like to see Bella Denton,' he said.

'She's not here at the moment,' said Karlene. 'She's visiting a friend at the hospital.'

He groaned. 'Not a bloke called Adam, is it?'

'That's right. Adam Green.'

'I only know him as Adam. I did him a favour.'

'Bella told us,' said Karlene. 'You delivered some flowers for him. Left them with our next-door neighbour.'

'Red roses. Wish I'd never set eyes on 'em.' Mick saw them in the vase and groaned. 'There they are!'

'Bella was really pleased with them,' said Suzie.

'She won't be so pleased when she gets home. They've got to go back.'

Suzie gulped. 'What!'

'It wasn't my fault,' he apologised. 'I honestly thought they were his to give. But they weren't. And that's why they've got to go back to the hospital. Smartish.'

'You've lost me,' said Karlene.

'Adam didn't buy the roses for your friend. He stole them from another patient.'

Karlene and Suzie looked at each other in astonishment.

'A woman in the ward opposite him,' said the porter. 'She was asleep when he nicked the flowers. When she woke up again, she raised the alarm. There'll be hell to pay if she doesn't get them back. And I'll be blamed. They cost a fortune.'

They felt sorry for him — Mick was a legendary figure at the hospital, well known for running errands for patients and staff alike. He was completely trustworthy. His image would be ruined if he was thought to be involved in the theft of some flowers.

'I must take them back,' he said. 'You do understand, don't you?'

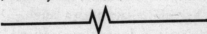

When Bella told her friends what had happened, they led her away at once. Gordy and Mark tried to comfort her. They could see she'd been very upset by the meeting with Adam.

'Let's get right out of this place,' said Gordy.

'You two go on ahead,' suggested Bella. 'I have to speak to someone else first.'

Mark was horrified. 'You're not going back to Adam?'

'No,' she said. 'But I'm hoping to catch Damian Holt. I know he comes off duty in Casualty about now.'

'You can't dump us for an Aussie!' complained Gordy.

'I need his advice.'

They reached a compromise. While they waited to take her home, Bella would have a quick word with her friend.

After a hard day's work in Casualty, he was pleased to see her welcoming face.

'Hi, Bella. Long time, no see.'

'Can you spare a minute?'

'Of course. What's the problem?'

'Drugs.'

He was taken aback. '*You've* been using drugs?'

'No, Damian, not me. I don't need a pill to turn me on.'

'That's true!' he said with a laugh.

'This is serious. It concerns a friend.'

'Tell me all.'

Damian led her into a quiet alcove and listened to her story. Bella told him about her meeting with Adam and described his behaviour in great detail.

'I'm out of my depth here, Damian,' she said. 'I need some guidance. What exactly is wrong with Adam?'

'I can only guess,' he said. 'But I'm not surprised that this all blew up at *Underworld*. Everybody seems to pop pills at that place. I've seen some of the results in Casualty.'

'With the same symptoms as Adam?'

'Not exactly. His is an interesting case.'

'Not when he turns on you, Damian. Nothing interesting in that, I can tell you. It's frightening.'

'Sudden mood swings are a feature of drug use. You obviously caught him at a bad time, Bella.'

'There's never been a good time with Adam.'

'Then you deserve full marks for hanging in there and trying to help him,' he said. 'You're right about the Rehab Unit. They only keep in acute cases. Adam obviously has a history of drug abuse. His system can't handle it.'

'Does that mean he's been on hard drugs?'

'Not necessarily. Even stimulants can have a disturbing effect on some people. Amphetamines, for instance. They're supposed to give you a buzz, make you really pumped up.'

'Adam certainly was at *Underworld*.'

'One dose lasts three or four hours,' he explained. 'For the average person, that is. But Adam is evidently not an average person.'

'What do you mean?'

'Heavy users can experience all kinds of unpleasant side-effects, Bella. Disturbed sleep, loss of appetite, feelings of acute anxiety and paranoia. That's if they're fairly normal to start with. Drugs warp the mind. If there are psychological problems already...'

'Then they can go out of control. Like Adam.'

'This is purely informed speculation, mind. I've never even met him.'

'Lucky you!' sighed Bella.

'If there's instability there,' said Damian, 'it may not be the result of taking drugs. If he was unstable before, the pills would have a particularly bad effect.'

Bella was very grateful to him. Damian had been patient and helpful. She gave him a hug out of gratitude. As they walked along the corridor together, she thought about Adam. Her first impulse was to turn and run away from him but Damian's words echoed in her ears. Adam might have psychological problems. In that case, he needed help and understanding. It would be cruel to abandon him now.

'Besides,' she said, chirpily, 'he's not all bad. Anyone who sends me a bouquet of red roses must have some good in him.'

She spoke too soon. Mick Morris was coming towards them, grinning sheepishly and holding something behind his back. She recognised the bouquet at once and grabbed at it. But the porter escaped her and scooted on down the corridor.

'Don't blame me!' he called. 'I have to take them back.'

'But Adam bought them for me!' she cried.

'That's what I thought. But he stole them from

120

another patient.' He vanished around a corner. 'Sorry!'

Bella was furious. Damian put a comforting arm around her.

'Not your day, is it?' he said.

CHAPTER TWELVE

Suzie surrendered her break that morning to visit Rainbow Ward. Still connected to the dialysis machine, Donna French was rather low but her mother was doing her best to keep up her daughter's morale. Suzie's arrival took the strain off Mrs French for a while.

'How're you feeling today?' Suzie asked.

'About the same,' said Donna.

'But all the better for seeing you,' added her mother.

'Have you made friends with any of the other children, Donna?'

'Some of them,' she said.

'Yes,' said Mrs French. 'They pop in and out all day long to show her their toys.'

'I've got my own toys,' said Donna, proudly.

She pointed to the box beside her. It contained dolls, a plastic flute, a few computer games, some simple jigsaws and a selection of well-thumbed books. Suzie felt a pang when she saw a nurse's uniform among the toys.

Suzie noticed that one of the books had a picture of a rabbit on the front. She caught Donna's eye — the little girl had a very special toy that the other children couldn't match. It had four legs and a white blob of a tail; Bobo's secret visits meant so much to her.

'Is Tim coming to see you today?' asked Suzie.

'I hope so.'

'But only at the proper time,' said Mrs French. 'I'm not having him sneaking off school again. He's in enough trouble already with his teachers. I've told Tim to come at lunchtime and after school. He's been turning up here at all hours.'

Suzie smiled. She had a feeling that Tim might go against his mother's orders. Visiting his sister was more important to Tim than anything. He'd willingly risk punishment at school in order to get to her during the day.

'You've got a marvellous collection of dolls,' said Suzie.

Donna grinned. 'They've all got names.'

'I bet I can guess what they are.'

'Go on, then.' She picked one up. 'Who's this?'

Suzie scrutinised the doll. 'Elaine!'

'No,' said Donna with a giggle. 'Rachel!'

'Let me try another,' said Suzie, picking up a rag doll with two silver buttons for eyes. 'I know — Priscilla!'

Donna giggled again. 'That's Sharon.'

Suzie was wide of the mark with each guess but she amused the young girl for several minutes. By the time she had to leave, Donna was in a much happier frame of mind.

'Can I come again?' asked Suzie.

Donna nodded, enthusiastically.

'Any time you like,' said Mrs French.

'But I'm not family.'

The mother winked. 'You are now.'

She followed Suzie to the door and gave her arm a squeeze.

'Thanks. You've really cheered her up.'

'Has the consultant seen her today?'

'Yes, he made his rounds first thing,' said Mrs French. 'Same old story. We have to wait for a donor. Someone who understands just how vital a kidney is.' She sighed. 'It's dreadful, Suzie. Waiting for someone to die and hoping they have a kidney donor card in their pocket.'

She went back to her daughter and Suzie waved goodbye. Donna's predicament had touched her; she was so brave and patient.

Suzie was about to go back upstairs when she heard a low whistle. She followed the sound along the corridor and around a corner. The sight which confronted her was no longer unusual.

Down on his hands and knees, Tim was peering under a trolley. He was whistling to his pet. The sound of Suzie's approach made him leap to his feet but he relaxed when he recognised a friend.

'I've come to see Donna,' he said.

'I know, Tim. I've just been in there myself.'

'Is she OK?'

'We had a good laugh together. But shouldn't

you be at school? Your mother told me you wouldn't sneak off again.'

'But Donna needs me!'

'What are you up to out here?'

'Nothing, nothing,' he said, quickly.

'Don't give me that,' warned Suzie. 'It's Bobo, isn't it? I told you not to bring him in again and you have. Where is he?'

'I don't know,' said Tim, spreading his arms in despair. 'Help me to find him, Suzie. *Please!* Before someone else does.'

When the lecture ended, Louise took her first close look at him. Concern clouded her face.

'Are you feeling all right, Mark?' she said.

'Yes thanks.'

'You don't look it.'

'I stayed up late last night,' he lied. 'Studying.'

'Don't overdo it,' Louise said.

'I'm not as clever as you, Louise. I have to put in more hours.' He felt slightly dizzy again and put his hand on the table to steady himself. 'I'll be fine when I wake up properly.'

'You must take more care of yourself.'

Her voice was so kind and she seemed so sympathetic that he felt touched. Louise was genuinely fond of him. It encouraged him to repeat his earlier invitation.

'I don't suppose you've had second thoughts? About the end-of-term dance?'

'Nothing could be further from my mind.'

'I'd really like to take you, Louise.'

'Maybe you will,' she said, 'if I decide to go.'

'You can't miss it — everybody will be there.'

'That's what I'm afraid of, Mark. I hate crowds. Even if I drop into the dance, I wouldn't stay all evening. Too many people. When it comes to social life, my ideal number is two.'

'And mine,' he said, seriously. 'Maybe we could go to the dance for an hour or so then steal away. Have a meal somewhere.'

'It's too soon to commit myself,' she said.

'Keep my offer in mind, will you?'

'I will, Mark. Thanks.'

'I wouldn't want to ask anyone else.'

Louise gave him an affectionate smile and he grinned. She picked up a pile of books from the table.

'I'll just take these back to the library,' she said.

'Let me do that for you.'

Mark's offer was well-intentioned but, unluckily, as he leant forward, his legs seemed to buckle and he fell against her. Louise was knocked backwards and her books flew out of her hands. They hit the floor with a thud.

'Sorry, Louise,' he said. 'I'll pick them up.'

'No!' she insisted. 'Just leave them, will you.'

He swayed over her. 'Sorry — it was an accident.'

'Have you been drinking?' she asked with disgust.

'No — of course not!' Mark was horrified she should think that.

'Then why can't you stand up properly?'

As Mark recovered, he stood bolt upright. 'Please, move back, Louise, let me get those books.'

'Don't touch them,' she snapped. 'Don't touch *anything* of mine.' She gathered up the fallen books. 'I can manage.'

She hurried out of the room. Mark felt well and truly snubbed.

———————/\/———————

Catherine White was more than a good tutor to Karlene; she'd become a friend as well. She was always available to offer help and advice to her students. Karlene called at the physiotherapist's office during her morning break.

'Mrs Tyc?' said Catherine.

'She came for treatment this week,' said Karlene. 'Virginia Tyc. That's her full name.'

'What was her problem?'

'A compound fracture of the radius. Her right arm. Came out of plaster a few days ago.'

'I remember her now,' said Catherine. 'A rather nervy woman in her twenties — too much make-up.

I'm hopeless on names and faces but I never forget an injury.'

Karlene decided to outline her theory — about how the injury might have been caused. Her tutor's eyes widened in disapproval.

'Do you have any proof of what you're saying?'

'Nothing definite, no.'

'Then don't you think you're jumping to conclusions?' asked her tutor, sternly.

'I just have this nagging feeling.'

'Control it, Karlene,' said Catherine. 'It's not part of your job to probe into people's marital difficulties. If we all did that, we'd begin to think there were wife-batterers behind every woman's broken arm or leg.'

'Then why did Mrs Tyc clam up on me, do you think?'

'Would you confide in a complete stranger? Especially someone as young as yourself?'

'As young and as inexperienced.'

'I wasn't going to say that.'

'It's true, Catherine. I'm still very green.'

'You'll be a good physio,' assured her tutor. 'As long as you stick to the job in hand. We're only a small cog in the medical machine. We help to keep the engine running.'

'In other words, it's none of my business.'

'You don't have time to *make* it your business.'

'But I've seen a woman in great distress.'

'The world is full of them, Karlene. That's the sad truth. They're called patients. Many of them are in a far worse condition than Mrs Tyc — she's one of the lucky ones.'

Catherine White was tall and slim in her white coat. Her dark hair was speckled with grey. She had a wealth of experience and a gift for passing it on to her students. Karlene decided there was no point in telling her about the meeting with Mrs Tyc in Casualty. Her advice would be the same —stay out of it.

As Karlene started to leave, she ventured another question.

'Have you ever dealt with a battered wife here?'

'Of course — several.'

'What did you advise?'

'I referred them to a social worker. If the patient is a victim of persistent assault, the first thing to do is get her away from the source of violence.'

'To a home for battered wives?'

'Well, a safe house of some kind,' said Catherine.

'Is there one close to this hospital?'

'Karlene...'

'I just wondered.'

'I have no idea,' said Catherine. 'Even if I did, I wouldn't tell you. The address is a closely-guarded secret.'

'Yes, of course.'

'What I can do is give you a contact number but

I'm not sure you need it.' She got up from her desk and put a hand on Karlene's shoulder. 'I appreciate your concern for Mrs Tyc but it's inappropriate here. You're not a social worker. Don't try to do their job for them.'

Karlene thanked her and left the office. She'd been given plenty of food for thought. Catherine White's advice had been sound and practical. Karlene was sorry she might have to ignore it.

Something kept drawing her back. Bella tried to put Adam out of her mind but his condition worried her. At the very least, she felt, she should ask how he was. She slipped across to Reception during her lunch hour to see what she could find out. A man came striding across to greet her.

'Bella!' he said.

'Hello, Mr Green.'

'I'm so glad I've bumped into you again. I really must apologise for my behaviour last time. Adam and I had just had a furious row. I'd reached the end of my tether.'

'That doesn't surprise me,' she said. 'I saw Adam myself later on. He seems very volatile.'

Philip Green was too embarrassed to talk in such a crowded area; he indicated a quieter part of the waiting room. They sat beside each other and talked in subdued voices.

'Have you seen him today?' asked Bella.

'Only for a short while,' said Adam's father.

'When are they going to discharge him?' asked Bella.

'They haven't decided yet.'

Bella remembered her chat with Damian. She braced herself to ask another question but she knew it might upset him.

'Has Adam ever had any mental problems?' she asked, quietly.

'Not really. He's always been highly-strung but that's a different thing altogether. Adam just doesn't handle stress very well. And he's had rather a lot of it.'

'Why did he abandon his course at the college?'

'Well, that's a case in point; it all got on top of him.'

'Adam told me he got bored.'

'That wasn't it, Bella,' he said. 'He worked hard at college — he even had some ambition in those days. But he couldn't stand the pace, not without Sarah, anyway.'

'Did she drop out as well?'

'I'm afraid so. Just after they broke up.' Mr Green became quite nostalgic. 'I often think it was the happiest time of Adam's life, that first term at college. Sarah was such a wonderful support to him.' He shook his head. 'If only she could offer some of that support now!'

Bella couldn't keep the news from him any longer. He had a right to know something so important in his son's life. Bella tried to break it as gently as possible.

'There's no hope of that, I'm afraid. I rang Sarah's home.'

'Did you?' he said with surprise. 'Why?'

'Because you seemed to put so much faith in her. So did Mrs Green. Both of you said how much Sarah had done for Adam, what she might still do. I felt sure she'd want to know what was happening to him.'

He sat on the edge of his seat. 'And did she? What did Sarah actually say?'

'I only spoke to her mother. It was a mistake. I felt I was intruding on their grief.'

'Grief?' His face went pale. 'What's happened, Bella?'

'Sarah died some weeks ago.'

He looked completely shattered. It was minutes before he could even speak. Tears began to slide down his cheeks.

'How... When?'

'I don't know any of the details, Mr Green. Her mother just told me the news and then put the phone down. After all, she didn't know who I was.'

'That's terrible,' he whispered. 'Sarah dying and we didn't even know about it! I can't believe it.' He stiffened suddenly and a worried look came into his eyes. 'This changes everything,' he said. 'Who's going to tell him? Who's going to tell Adam. He'll fall apart.'

CHAPTER THIRTEEN

'When did you last see him?' asked Suzie.

'In the ward sister's office,' said Tim French.

'What on earth were you doing in there?'

'Hiding — from her. Bobo jumped out of my pocket,' said Tim. 'And before I could stop him, he'd raced off down the corridor. I went after him and I was still looking for him when you found me.'

'Be grateful it was me and not someone from hospital security. If they'd caught sight of a rabbit, they'd have thrown you and him straight out.'

They were talking as they looked into every room, alcove and cupboard they passed. Tim even checked a ventilation duct to see if it was big enough for a rabbit the size of Bobo. Their search was fruitless.

Suzie remembered Bobo had escaped once before.

'Where did he go last time?' she asked Tim.

'Up to the next floor. I found him in a storeroom.'

'Suppose it'd been a laundry room,' said Suzie with alarm. 'An animal in amongst all that linen.'

'Bobo is very clean.' insisted Tim.

'Everything in here has to be sterile,' said Suzie.

'He wouldn't leave any marks.'

'Bobo's a rabbit — he might have fleas.'

'We wash him regular. And spray him with some stuff.'

'I'm sure you take great care of him,' said Suzie. 'But this isn't the place for a pet, Tim. Don't bring him again, OK?'

'But Donna asked to see him,' said the boy. 'It's not much fun being stuck on that machine. Donna's afraid she might never come out of hospital. Bobo cheers her up.'

'I'm sure he does but enough is enough. I'll explain to her myself. The risk is too great. Look at the trouble Bobo's caused already.'

'He likes to play hide-and-seek, that's all.'

'Well, he can't do it in a hospital,' said Suzie firmly. 'Find him and take him home. Do you understand?'

A reluctant nod. 'Yeah — all right.'

'Otherwise, you may lose him altogether.'

Tim nodded sadly. Having gone to great lengths to get Bobo there, he'd relaxed for a second and the animal had made his bid for freedom. There were far too many places for him to hide — Tim might never find him.

Suzie was feeling very guilty now. She should have been much firmer about the pet rabbit being brought into the hospital. Allowing Tim to smuggle it in again, she'd appeared to agree with what he was doing. That could land her in serious trouble. To make amends, she had to find Bobo as quickly as possible and get him off the premises once and for all.

When they'd searched several corridors, she paused.

'Are you certain he's still on this floor?'

'He's got to be,' said Tim

They turned aside as two nurses came out of a ward and strolled past. Suzie gulped as she saw the swing doors shut. If Bobo got loose among patients, he would cause a mild riot.

'Where *is* he?' she whispered, anxiously.

A flash of white appeared at the end of the corridor.

'There!' yelled Tim. 'Come here, Bobo!'

As Tim sprinted down the corridor, the rabbit vanished around a corner. Suzie followed as fast as she could safely allow herself to go. The chase was on.

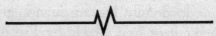

Bella sat in silence beside him for several minutes. Philip Green was still trying to absorb the impact of the news. When he eventually spoke, his voice was a hoarse whisper.

'I feel very sorry for her family,' he said.

'Did you know them well?'

'No, Bella. We only met a few times. But they were nice people. Adam seemed to get on with them.' He stirred guiltily. 'I just wish I'd known about Sarah. I'd have got in touch with them. I'd have gone to the funeral.'

'That may not have been wise,' said Bella, softly.

'Why?'

'When I mentioned Adam's name over the phone, Mrs Green was very upset. She obviously feels bitter about him. If you'd shown up at Sarah's funeral...'

'Yes, yes,' he agreed, nodding. 'I'd hate to have caused any additional suffering. I didn't realise she held anything against Adam. But I'd still like to know how Sarah died. She was so young — it's a tragedy.'

'When did you last see her, Mr Green?'

'Three of four months ago.'

'Was that after she'd broken up with Adam?'

'Yes,' he said. 'I was in my car, driving along the High Street. I caught a glimpse of Sarah, standing on a corner with two or three other people. I recognised one of them — a boy called Jez.'

Bella sat up. 'Jez Halliday?'

'That's right. Do you know him?'

'Yes, unfortunately.'

'He was at school with Adam and Sarah. Not that you'd call him a friend. They avoided him like the plague. That's why I was so surprised to see Sarah with him. Especially after what she'd once said about Jez.'

'Go on,' said Bella.

'She'd had an argument with Adam one night, at the house. I couldn't help overhearing. "Keep away from Jez!" she shouted. "He's a maniac!" Those were her exact words.'

'I'd go along with those sentiments!' said Bella.

'So what was she *doing* with him?'

'I don't know, Mr Green. How did Sarah look?'

'That was the other thing,' he said. 'She looked so dowdy. Almost neglected. Sarah was usually very smart. She took a pride in her appearance. But she was just wearing a sweatshirt and a pair of old jeans. To be honest, I wasn't even sure it was her at first.'

'Did she see you?' wondered Bella.

'I think so. I slowed the car down and waved. Sarah pretended not to notice. But Jez certainly did.' His voice hardened. 'He made a crude gesture at me.'

'Adam told me Sarah had always hated Jez,' said Bella.

'That's what I thought - until I saw them together.' He ran a hand through his hair. 'The truth is I've put the incident right out of my mind - until now. I prefer to remember Sarah as she was when we knew her. Friendly, open and full of fun. That was the real Sarah Baker.' A stab of remorse made him wince. 'I just can't believe she's dead.'

'It shook me when I heard,' confessed Bella.

Mr Green came to a decision and got to his feet.

'I must find out the details,' he said. 'I'll have to

ring her home.' Before she could speak, he raised his hand. 'Don't worry, Bella. I'll be very tactful. But I can't rest until I know. Is there a public telephone in here?'

'On the far wall,' she said, pointing.

'Thank you, Bella. And thanks for all you've done. I'm sorry you've got bogged down in our family problems. Look, I'm sure you have lots to do. Don't let me keep you.'

'I'm waiting until you've made that phone call, Mr Green,' she said. 'I'm as anxious to know the truth about Sarah as you are.'

———————∧———————

Gordy brought two cups of coffee to the table and sat down opposite Karlene. The canteen was more subdued than usual. They didn't need to shout above the din for once.

'So what happened, Kar?' he said.

'She rang me this morning.'

'What did Mrs Tyc say?' he asked.

'Very little,' replied Karlene. 'She was really nervous. She just gabbled her message and put the phone down.'

'So what will you do?'

'Exactly what she asked me. Go and see her at this place she works in.' Gordy frowned with disapproval. 'It's the least I can do, Gordy. The woman's asking for my help.'

'But you're not the person to give it, Kar.'

'Who else is there?'

'Her GP, her parish priest, her best friend; anybody but you.' Gordy sipped his coffee. 'You're not trained to handle this kind of situation.'

'Mrs Tyc has asked for my help. I can't refuse her.'

'You must - learn a lesson from poor old Bel.'

'That's quite different, Gordy.'

'No, it's not. She got too involved and look where it's landed her. In a horrible mess. She's looking over her shoulder all the time in case that Jez character crawls out and jumps on her again.'

'There's no comparison with this situation.'

'Of course, there is,' he argued. 'Supposing Mrs Tyc's husband *does* knock her around? He's not going to like it if you try to protect her. He could turn nasty, Kar. Have you thought about that? He could come after you.'

'I'm not afraid of him,' she said, firmly. 'And if you don't stand up to bullies, they go on bullying. Besides, all I've agreed to is a private meeting with his wife. She wants to talk.'

'All right. Play the Good Samaritan, if you must. But don't say I didn't warn you.'

'Mrs Tyc sounded desperate over the phone. I have to go.'

'Fair enough. Do you want some moral support?'

'No thanks, Gordy. This is something I must do on my own. If I arrive with you, she'll go all silent on me.' She patted his arm. 'You stay on guard for Bella. She really needs you.'

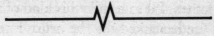

'Why didn't you *tell* me you were coming across here?' said Mark.

'I only came to enquire about Adam.'

'But that slob might have jumped on you again.'

'In broad daylight?'

'That didn't stop him the last time, Bella.'

'I was safe enough,' she assured him. 'There are far too many people about. Even Jez isn't stupid enough to approach me in the middle of a crowd.'

Mark was glad he'd found her in Reception. The search for Bella had clearly made him anxious. He was swaying slightly and the buzzing in his ears was worse than ever.

'Are you all right?' she said. 'You look very pale.'

'I'm fine now I've tracked you down.'

'I was perfectly safe. And very glad I came here, because I bumped into Mr Green,' she said. 'And I managed tell him about Sarah. I've been carrying that news around for ages. I was really pleased to get it off my chest.'

'How did Mr Green take it?'

'He was shattered, Mark. He was very fond of

Sarah. It was a terrible blow for him.' She took a deep breath. 'It's going to be an even bigger blow for Adam.'

'Who's going to tell him?'

'His father. He's up there right now. Mr Green couldn't understand why he wasn't told about Sarah's death. Why Adam didn't even know. It was as if her parents had hushed the whole thing up. I understand why now.'

'What do you mean?'

'Mr Green spoke to Sarah's mother on the phone. She was very evasive at first. She wasn't keen to talk about it; and still bitter about Adam. But Mr Green's very gentle and persuasive. He finally managed to get her to tell him everything. Sarah died from a drug overdose.'

Bella took him up to the hospital canteen for lunch. She was worried about him. Mark hardly touched his food. He usually had a healthy appetite. She badgered him until he told her about the problems he'd been having.

'Why don't you go straight back to bed?' she suggested.

'I feel fine, Bella.'

'That's just not true. I can tell by looking at you. At least go and see your GP this evening.'

'Maybe,' said Mark. 'I'll think about it.'

'Headaches, a hearing problem, dizzy spells. How many more symptoms do you need? You're ill.'

'Not all the time. It sort of comes and goes.'

'So you've got some kind of intermittent disease,' she said. 'Have it checked out. Or it may get worse.'

'I'd just feel a bit of a fraud, Bella. Going to the doctor when there's really nothing wrong with me.'

'You told me your knees buckled under you this morning; that you collapsed against Louise.'

'That's right. I did.'

'Is that normal?'

'Of course not.'

'Then do something about it.'

'I'll take some more paracetemol.'

'That obviously isn't working — your symptoms are still there. How many dizzy spells have you had?' she asked.

He ran his hands through his hair. 'About three — or four.'

'One would be enough to ring my alarm bell, Mark. If I had two, I'd be off to the surgery to see my GP.'

'I will go, I promise.'

Mark was glad he'd talked to Bella. Her advice was always practical. When he'd told her about the incident with Louise's books, she'd been very sympathetic.

'Every girl wants a man to fall at her feet,' she said. 'But not in *that* way. Louise must have been very surprised.'

'She was mad at me.'

'Didn't you explain you'd had a dizzy spell?'

'I didn't get the chance.'

'So what's Louise going to think?'

'That I'm stupid and clumsy.'

'But you're not!'

'She'll never come to the end-of-term dance with me now,' he sighed. 'Louise will be afraid I'll tread all over her toes and then spill wine down her dress.'

Bella put a consoling hand on his arm. It was rare to find Mark in such a depressed mood. Of the five friends, he was the most stable character. The others usually turned to him because they knew they could rely on him for solid support. For once, it was Mark himself who needed help.

'Shall I speak to Louise?'

'No, no,' he said in alarm. 'Don't do that.'

'But I could explain what really happened when you dropped those books. You don't want her thinking you were drunk.'

'I'll sort it out my way, Bella.'

'It might be better coming from me.'

Mark doubted that. Bella was a good friend but he didn't want her to talk to Louise about him. It would only make matters worse. Bella's relationships with boyfriends tended to be short but lively. Mark could imagine the kind of thing she might say to Louise — it made him blush. Whatever their problems, he and Louise could only solve them together.

'Thanks all the same,' he said. 'But the answer is no.'

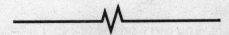

Suzie and Tim had a problem. Bobo was much better at hide-and-seek than either of them. All they ever caught was an occasional glimpse of him as he left one refuge to dash to another. Their hunt for the white rabbit was hampered by various people who walked up and down the corridors. Suzie and her young friend had to pretend they were just chatting.

When the coast was clear, they resumed their search.

Suzie felt dejected and flopped into a plastic chair.

'I'm whacked,' she said, panting.

'We almost caught him,' said Tim.

'We didn't even get within three metres of Bobo.'

'He'll give in sooner or later.'

'Well, I won't be here to see it, I'm afraid,' she said. 'I've got a lecture in ten minutes. Thanks to Bobo, I missed my lunch.'

'Sorry — he can be naughty sometimes.'

'I don't blame him. The poor animal must be frightened being here in strange surroundings. He just bolted.' She looked sternly at Tim. 'The person to blame is you, Tim. You're the one who brought him in here.'

'I know, I know.'

'If and when you find Bobo...'

'He goes straight home and stays there.'

'Promise?'

'Yeah.'

'Right. You carry on the search. I'll race down to Reception and grab a sandwich from the shop.'

'See if they've got any salad sandwiches - Bobo likes them.'

Suzie was getting really fed up. 'I'm buying food because I'm hungry. Not because I want to give it to a rabbit!' She stopped and changed her mind. 'Wait a minute. You may be on to something there.'

'Bobo's hungry as well,' said Tim.

'If we offer him food, he may come back.'

'Yeah — lettuce. He loves nibbling lettuce.'

'It's on its way, Tim,' she said, making for the stairs. 'I don't care if he takes the food out of my mouth, it'll be worth it to catch the little so-and-so.'

'Suzie...'

'Yes,' she called over her shoulder.

'I haven't had lunch either. I don't suppose you'd get me a bag of crisps?'

Suzie stopped and looked round. Tim grinned at her.

'Salt and vinegar flavour.'

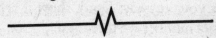

Karlene learnt a lot from watching Catherine White at work. The physiotherapist had such a relaxed and confident manner. She knew how to put the patients at ease. By the time she'd finished taking them through their exercises, they looked much better. A session with Catherine White was always productive.

Karlene stole a moment alone with her tutor.

'I don't know how you do it,' she said.

'Do what, Karlene?'

'Talk to them as a group yet make each patient think that you're speaking directly to him or her.'

'That comes with practice,' said Catherine. 'And a lot of trial and error. Know your patients, that's the secret. Mrs Lomax will do anything I ask her but Mr Fenton needs to be coaxed into some of the exercises. Mrs Voisey, on the other hand, has more or less to be forced into it. She's inclined to be lazy.'

'But you didn't *seem* to be forcing her.'

'Gentle pressure. Constantly applied. You'll learn.'

'I hope so,' said Karlene.

Her tutor was about to walk away when she remembered something. Putting her hand into the pocket of her white coat, she took out a slip of paper.

'I don't know if you still want this but I wrote it down for you, anyway. Don't show it around. It's that contact number we discussed.'

Karlene thought about her meeting with Mrs Tyc.

'Thanks,' she said. 'I'll take it. Just in case.'

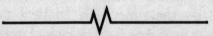

They were both waiting for her. When Bella was leaving the college of nurses, she found Philip and Judith Green in the hall. They looked up anxiously as she approached. Bella nodded to them and asked what they were doing there.

'Sorry to impose on you again,' said Mr Green. 'But we had to speak to you.'

'Yes,' added Judith. 'My husband rang me and told me the tragic news about Sarah. I felt I had to come. We've been at the hospital all afternoon.'

He gave a tired smile. 'My school will begin to wonder where I am. The Case of the Vanishing Headmaster.'

'They'll understand, Philip,' said his wife. 'You had to be here. Adam had to be told the truth.'

Bella wanted to know how the visit with his son had gone but it was too public a place to ask. Student nurses were milling about and Mark was waiting to escort her home. She suggested they went outside. The walk across the car park gave them some privacy. Mark stayed a discreet distance behind.

'How did Adam cope with the news?' asked Bella.

'Not very well,' admitted Philip. 'He refused to believe it at first. He accused me of inventing the story just to make him feel guilty. I think he was shocked to realise just how far he and Sarah had drifted apart — that he'd lost touch so completely he didn't even know something as important as this.'

'Sarah was on drugs as well,' sighed Judith. 'It's heart-breaking. She was the last person in the world you'd have expected to get drawn into that world.'

'Not according to Adam,' said her husband. 'They'd tried cannabis together at college. Sarah was the one who wanted to experiment with other drugs. Adam was against the idea. It was one of the things that pushed them apart.' He gave a hopeless shrug. 'Ironic, isn't it. Sarah's parents blame him for introducing her to drugs but it may well have been the other way around.'

'Adam must have been devastated by the news,' said Bella.

They nodded.

'Did it make him angry or violent?'

'Not with me, Bella. But I could see that he was very angry with himself. For not being there to save Sarah.'

'He's hardly in a condition to do that,' observed Judith.

'Don't rub it in,' said Mr Green, wincing.

'It must have been a nightmare for you, Mr Green. Did you mention Jez at any stage?'

'Yes, I told him about seeing Jez and Sarah that time. That really made him mad. He began to shout and get upset. The nurse had to calm him down.'

Bella could imagine the scene only too well. She was glad she hadn't been the one to break the sad news to Adam. She wouldn't have felt confident of handling the situation.

'We just have to hope some good comes out of it all,' said Judith. 'Drugs can kill. Now that Adam's seen that with his own eyes, it might make him realize the dangers.'

'In time, maybe,' said her husband. 'In time.'

'What happens now?' asked Bella.

'He wants to see you, Bella. I don't know why but Adam was very insistent. You're an outsider. You're not part of this mess. Maybe he thinks you can be more objective about it all than we can.' He smiled wearily again. 'Also, he likes you. And trusts you.'

Bella hesitated. She was reluctant to visit Adam while he was in such a disturbed state. He'd been unsettled enough on her previous visit but he might be much worse this time.

'We know it's a lot to ask of you,' said Judith.

'But we'd take it as a very big favour,' added Philip. 'To Adam — and to us. Will you go, Bella? Please.'

She thought it over. 'All right,' she said at length. 'If it'll help, I'll go up there straightaway.'

They were extremely grateful and followed her back into the main hospital. Mark, too, kept her in sight. Bella went up in the lift to the Third Floor. When she reached the East Wing, she reported to the reception desk.

'I've come to see Adam Green,' she told them.

The nurse consulted a chart in front of her.

'That's not possible, I'm afraid.'

'But he asked me to come and see him.'

'Adam's not receiving any more visitors.'

'But he asked his father to get me,' said Bella. 'Adam needs to talk to me — urgently.'

'He must have changed his mind,' said the nurse.

'He's refusing to see anybody. I can't let you in. No visitors.'

Bella was flabbergasted.

CHAPTER FIFTEEN

Mark was waiting in Reception with growing discomfort. There was a dull ache inside his head and some nasal congestion. What really disturbed him was his right ear. The slight deafness had been replaced by a troubling echo. Whenever he picked up a sound, it seemed to reverberate in his ear. Mark felt as if he had a tiny bell attached to his eardrum. Its ring was worrying.

'Where is she, Mark? We're supposed to be guarding her. Remember? I saw you coming in here with Bella.'

'She went upstairs to see Adam again.'

'That girl is a glutton for punishment!'

Gordy looked more closely at his friend.

'You're as white as a sheet, Marco.'

'I do feel a bit rough, to be honest.'

'Right,' decided Gordy. 'You're off duty, mate. Go to the surgery straightaway. You need a doctor.'

'I'll feel fine in a minute.'

'Do as you're told. I can take care of Bella.'

'Thanks, Gordy. I'll see you later.'

Mark hated having to leave but he knew now he should see a doctor. But as he tried to walk across Reception, his body wouldn't respond. His head felt heavy, his ear was like an echo chamber and his stomach was heaving. It was almost like being seasick. As he tried to force himself on, he staggered drunkenly for a few paces, then pitched forwards on to the marble floor.

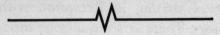

Suzie was disappointed to see him still on his own.

'Haven't you found Bobo yet?' she asked.

'I found him lots of times,' said Tim, sadly. 'I just haven't been able to catch him.'

'But you've been here all afternoon.'

'On and off. People kept coming. This bloke caught me peering into the kitchens and got nasty with me. He's been back a few times.'

'A security guard?'

'Yeah. In a peaked cap. Then there was Mum.'

'What did she want?'

'She wanted to know why I hadn't been in to see Donna. That's why I come here. To visit my sister. So I did.'

Suzie was alarmed. 'Bobo could have gone up or down the stairs during that time!'

'I still think he's on this floor,' said the small boy.

'Then catch him, Tim!'

'He's too fast.'

'I wish Donna had a tortoise for a pet!' she moaned. 'Or a goldfish. They can't swim away.'

'Neither can Bobo.'

Suzie sighed and looked up and down the corridor. It had been a long day but she felt she couldn't leave as long as the white rabbit was at large. Tim was only a child. He needed her help.

'What happened to my lettuce sandwich?' she said.

'I ate it.'

'But I bought it for Bobo.'

'He didn't like the smell of it. He only has crisp lettuce at home. Yours was soggy.'

Suzie laughed involuntarily.

'Look at us. Standing here in one of the most modern hospitals in Britain, discussing the eating habits of a rabbit. How was Donna, by the way?'

'She's not very happy about that machine she's on. They keep telling her it's like an artificial kidney but she wants a real one. Like everyone else.'

'I bet she was glad to see you. Will you get into trouble for missing school?'

'It doesn't bother me.'

'Ask your mother to write a letter. To explain.'

'What?' said the boy. 'That I spent most of the day chasing Bobo round the hospital? My teachers'd love that.'

'Do they know your sister is in hospital?'

'Yeah. Everyone does. It was in the paper — about her kidney.'

'Did they appeal for a donor?' asked Suzie.

'I think so.' The boy blinked. 'Don't know much about it really. I'm still not sure what a kidney really is. Except that I've got two of my own. All I know is, Donna needs a new one. To save her life. That's what it said in the paper.'

Tim spoke in a matter-of-fact tone but he was worried about his sister. If her case had got so much publicity, her condition had to be very serious. Suzie stopped feeling irritated with him. Like the rest of his family, he deserved her sympathy.

'Let's start all over again, shall we?' she said.

'Ready when you are, Suzie.'

'Let's go!'

But their long wait was nearly over. As they began to walk away from the stairs, they heard shouting in the distance. Heavy footsteps were running towards them. They looked down the corridor in time to see a white rabbit come hurtling around the corner.

'Bobo!' exclaimed Tim.

'Grab him!' ordered Suzie.

'Come back, you little devil!' roared an unseen man.

Tim moved with remarkable speed. He dived on Bobo and rolled over before jumping to his feet again. The squirming rabbit was quickly put into the pocket of his coat. When the security guard came around the corner, the animal was out of sight.

The guard lumbered towards them with his chest heaving.

'Where did that rabbit go?' he demanded.

'That way?' said Suzie, pointing to the stairs.

'Up or down?'

'Up.'

The guard swore under his breath then mounted the steps as fast as he could. Suzie swung round to Tim.

'Get him out of here. Fast!'

'Can't I take him in to see Donna first?'

'No! It's too dangerous. I'll go and see her. You take Bobo home.'

'Come on, then,' said Tim, slipping a hand inside his coat to stroke Bobo. 'You must be starving. Let's go home and find some *real* lettuce.'

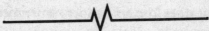

The launderette was a long, narrow establishment less than a mile from the hospital. Two rows of washing machines stood back-to-back down the middle of the room. Plastic chairs faced each other down both walls. Several of the machines were in action — their motors whirring.

A few people were waiting for their washing but others had left it there to be picked up later. When Karlene walked in, Virginia Tyc was giving a customer her change. One of the machines was coming to the end of its spin cycle. When the thunderous noise stopped, Mrs Tyc opened the glass-fronted door and unloaded the washing into a plastic basket. She put it aside for collection.

'Have I come at an awkward time?' said Karlene.

'Not really.'

Virginia Tyc went behind the little counter and Karlene followed her. They would not be overheard. The hum of the machines would keep their conversation private.

The poor woman was as embarrassed as ever.

'Thank you,' she said. 'For coming.'

Mrs Tyc checked to see that nobody was listening. She went on.

'He's not such a bad man,' she said. 'My husband. Most of the time he's quite kind to me.'

'Go on,' said Karlene.

'But he does lose his temper sometimes. He can't help it.'

'That's no excuse, Mrs Tyc,' said Karlene. 'What happens when your husband loses his temper?'

'He can turn violent. And then somebody gets hurt.'

'Just you? Or the children as well?'

'Oh, just me,' she said, scandalised by the suggestion. 'My husband loves the children. He'd never lay a finger on them. I swear it.'

'But he does hit you from time to time?'

A long pause. 'Yes.'

'Was he responsible for your broken arm?'

'Yes.'

'What about that gash on your hand?'

Suddenly, a look of fear came on to the woman's face.

'I can't talk about that,' she said. 'He'd kill me.'

'Are you so afraid of him, Mrs Tyc?'

'I've told you too much already.'

'What are you going to do about your husband?'

The woman spread her hands and shrugged hopelessly.

'What can I do?'

'Report him.'

'Go to the police, you mean? Oh, no. I couldn't do that.'

'Then it'll go on and on. Is that what you want?'

Mrs Tyc shook her head. The telephone rang and she snatched it up. The caller asked her what time the launderette closed. When she'd given the information, Mrs Tyc put down the receiver. Her eyes darted around nervously.

'There's nothing I can do.'

'Yes, there is,' insisted Karlene. 'You could leave him.'

'But he's my husband!'

'Does that give him the right to break your arm?'

'Well...no.'

'Then make sure it can't happen again,' said Karlene.

Virginia Tyc was overwhelmed by the very idea.

'I couldn't walk out on him,' she shuddered.

'Why not?'

'He'd come after me.'

'Only if he knew where you were.'

'He'd be bound to know that.'

'No, he wouldn't, Mrs Tyc. Not if you were in a safe house. There are lots of women in your position. Homes have been set up to look after them. Places where husbands and boyfriends can't find the women they've attacked.'

'What about my children?'

'You'd take them with you.'

'They'd be allowed as well?'

'Of course.'

A customer came in and left some washing. Virginia Tyc loaded it into a machine and pressed the button to start it. As she came back to the counter, she was thoughtful. Leaving her husband was a huge step to take and she wasn't sure she had the courage to take it. Then she glanced down at her bandaged hand. It was still throbbing, painfully.

'Do you know where one of these homes is?'

'No,' admitted Karlene. 'But I've got a contact number. Ring this and ask for advice.'

She held out the slip of paper which Catherine White had given to her. Mrs Tyc looked at it nervously. Then reached out and took the paper from Karlene's hand.

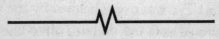

Bella came down to Reception again. Gordy was waiting impatiently for her outside the lift.

'That was a short visit.'

'Adam wouldn't see me. The nurse turned me away.'

'That might be a blessing in disguise, Bel,' he said. 'Anyway, I'm glad you've come back. Something's happened. Mark's been taken ill.'

'What's wrong with him?'

'We don't know yet. He just went out like a light. Fell flat on his face in the middle of Reception.'

'Poor Mark!'

'They've taken him through to Casualty. I must go and see him, Bel. I can't leave Mark on his own in that state.'

'Of course. Off you go. Straightaway,' Bella insisted.

'I hate deserting you like this.'

'I've got Mr and Mrs Green for company,' she said. 'I'd rather come with you but I can't leave now. They need moral support. I'll sit it out with them for an hour or so. In case Adam changes his mind.'

'Whatever you do, don't leave the building.'

'Promise.'

'I'll come back for you.'

'Give Mark my love.'

'I will.'

She waved as Gordy hurried off to Casualty. The news about Mark had upset him. Gordy was hoping to be a doctor one day, and he felt he should have spotted the signs of Mark's illness before.

Bella glanced over at the Greens who were involved in another argument. They weren't expecting her for some time yet and didn't notice her. She felt the need of some coffee before she rejoined them. There was a vending machine in the far corner of Reception. Fumbling in her purse for change, Bella walked towards it.

As she tried to insert the first coin, a strong hand caught her wrist and pulled her roughly into a doorway. Bella spun round to find her face only inches away from Jez Halliday's He had a crazy look in his eyes.

'Remember me?' he said with a leer.

'Go away!'

Before she could scream, his hand covered her mouth.

'Take me to Adam!' he ordered. 'Now!'

Bella was petrified. Jez had taken her completely by surprise. More than fifty people were within earshot in Reception but she couldn't reach any of them. She was dragged swiftly along the corridor to the emergency exit at the far end. Jez lifted the bar with his arm then used his full weight to push the door open. Bella was yanked unceremoniously through it. The metal door clanged shut behind them.

Jez glared at her as he issued a dire warning.

'If you try to shout — you're dead!'

He took his hand from her mouth. Bella let out a gasp of relief. He'd been hurting her.

'Which floor?' he snarled.

'Third.'

'Lead the way.'

He gave her a shove and Bella began to climb the concrete staircase. Jez kept a restraining hand on her arm so that she couldn't make a run for it. Bella didn't have the urge to escape. She was too frightened. Her previous encounters with Jez had been unpleasant. But this one was terrifying. Jez looked deranged. His face was contorted, his eyes glittered unnaturally. A strange power seemed to be running through him.

Bella made an effort to remain calm. Her survival depended on it. When they reached the first floor, she turned to face him. She tried to sound calm but her voice quavered a little.

'There's no point in you going there,' she said. 'Adam won't see you.'

'Yes, he will.'

'He won't see any visitors. They just turned me away. You won't get anywhere near him.'

'Who's going to stop me?'

'The ward sister.'

He laughed, mockingly. 'Keep moving.'

'I passed on your message,' said Bella, holding her ground. 'Adam said he didn't owe you anything.'

'Then he's lying.'

'He reckons he settled his debt.'

'He can never do that.' He prodded her. 'Get going.'

'No!' she said, defying him.

He pushed her against the wall and snatched something from inside his coat. Bella was horrified. He had a gun. Jez held the end of the barrel against the side of her head. She shivered.

'Do as you're told!' he ordered.

Bella climbed the concrete steps numb with terror.

'Stop treating me as if I'm an invalid,' said Mark.

'But that's exactly what you are,' said Suzie.

'You keeled over,' reminded Gordy. 'Healthy people stay on their feet. They don't nose-dive on to floor.'

Mark was glad to see them when he left the doctor in Casualty. His friends were sitting in the waiting room. When they saw he was still unsteady, they helped him to a chair.

'What did the doctor say?' asked Suzie.

'I've got a touch of labyrinthitis.'

'A touch of *what*?'

'Labyrinthitis.'

'It's an infection of the inner ear,' said Gordy, airily. 'The labyrinth is just that. A maze of ducts and canals that control hearing and balance.'

'I had an echoing sound in my ear,' explained Mark. 'Then my balance went completely. I felt dreadful. It's been coming on for some time. The doctor told me to have a couple of days in bed until it passes off. He's prescribed some pills.'

'Right,' said Gordy. 'Let's get you straight home.'

'Mark's in no state to walk,' said Suzie.

'I might make it with a bit of help.'

'You're ill,' she said, solicitously. 'You've punished yourself enough, struggling on when you were so poorly. Gordy can slip home to fetch his car. That's the only way you're leaving this hospital.'

'Good idea,' said Gordy, rising to his feet. 'Aren't you glad I rounded up Suzie to lend a hand?

You sit tight and the Robbins Taxi Service will leap into action.'

Mark looked flustered. 'What about Bella?'

'Don't worry about her.'

'But we were supposed to be looking after her, Gordy.'

'She's staying at the hospital for a while,' he said. 'She's in good hands.'

———— ⋀ ————

Bella felt as if she was on fire. As Jez pushed her up the steps, she had an attack of prickly heat. It made her twist and writhe. Her mind was racing madly. Adam was still in a delicate state. The last thing he needed was to have Jez coming after him with a gun. She tried to think of ways to stop Jez reaching him.

When they reached the third floor, she stopped.

'How much does Adam owe you?' she asked.

'That's my business.'

'He's got no money on him. I can tell you that.'

'I'm not after money.'

'Then what are you after?'

She looked up into his dark, evil eyes. Jez snarled. He swayed slightly. She wondered if he was drunk. There was no smell of alcohol on his breath but he was under the influence of something powerful.

'Leave him alone,' she implored.

'You've got to be joking!'

'Adam's not well.'

'Big deal!'

'Wait until they let him out of here.'

'I need to see him now.'

'You hate him, don't you?' said Bella.

He bared his teeth in a grin. 'Yeah.'

'You've always hated him. Because of Sarah.'

'Sarah?' The grin vanished. 'How d'you know about her?'

'Adam told me. She despised you.'

'That's not true!' he snarled.

'Sarah belonged to him. She wouldn't look at you.'

'That's what you think!'

'According to Adam, she wouldn't even—'

'Shut up!' he yelled, putting a hand over her mouth again. 'Don't even mention her name. It's got nothing to do with you. This is strictly between me and Adam.'

Bella tried to move his hand away but his grip was too strong. He pushed her slowly backwards until she was tight up against the brick wall. The pain made Bella wince.

'I want Adam,' he grunted. 'Where is he?'

Bella had no choice. With the gun in the small of her back, she led the way along the corridor towards East Wing. Whenever a nurse or a porter went past, she wanted to cry out for help but the feel of cold steel against her ribs kept her silent. Jez Halliday was in no mood to be crossed. Bella was certain he would use the gun if need be.

When they reached the ward, the nurse was behind the reception desk. The ward sister was talking to her. Jez stayed behind Bella so that his gun would be hidden. Sister Poole looked up at them. She regarded Jez with disapproval. Her tone was polite but firm.

'Did you want something?' she asked.

'Yeah,' he said. 'Adam Green.'

'He's not seeing visitors this evening, I'm afraid.'

'Tell him it's me — Jez.'

'There's no point,' she said. 'Besides, he's only allowed to see family and close friends. I'm not sure you fit into either category.'

'Come back tomorrow,' suggested Bella, eager to escape.

'Get him out here now!' insisted Jez.

'I'm sorry,' said the sister. 'But it's quite out of the question. You've wasted your time.'

'Get him out here!'

He made a threatening gesture with his fist but Sister Poole didn't flinch. Her tone hardened slightly.

'If you don't leave, I'll have to call security.'

'Go on, then.'

'You'd be much better advised to leave quietly.'

'Nobody's shifting me from here.'

'Now, listen, young man...'

'Don't push him,' warned Bella.

'I'll handle this,' said the sister, easily. 'Visiting is strictly controlled on this ward. We can't have any Tom, Dick or Harry wandering in.' She gave a dismissive smile. 'Adam won't see you this evening. Or anybody else. So you'll just have to come back another time.'

But Jez wasn't listening. He was staring over her shoulder at a sign on the door. His eyes ignited as a new plan formed. Everything else went out of his mind. He laughed, strangely, then pointed to the Pharmacy.

'Give me the key to that room,' he demanded.

'I'll do nothing of the kind!'

'Give it to me or there'll be big trouble!'

'You can't go in there,' said Bella. 'It's where they keep all the medication. Restricted access.'

'I want the key!' he growled.

'Who is this man, Bella?' said Sister Poole.

'His name is Jez Halliday.'

'Is he a friend of yours?'

'No way!'

'Listen, Mr Halliday,' said the sister, reasonably. 'This is a hospital. We have rules here. Medication is only issued on a doctor's prescription. No unauthorised person is allowed into the pharmacy. I'm sure you understand.'

'Open that door for me!' he ordered.

'I can't do that, I'm afraid.'

'Open it!' he said, glaring belligerently.

Sister Poole showed no fear. She was used to aggressive behaviour from some of her patients. Bella was scared. She was amazed at the sister's apparent calmness.

'Come into my office,' suggested Sister Poole.

'No,' he snapped.

'I'll send for a doctor and he can discuss your problem with you. If you need medication, he can prescribe it.'

'I know what I need.' He pointed his finger again. 'And it's in there.'

'Step into my office just for a moment.'

'No, it's a trick.'

'Now, look, Mr Halliday...'

'I'm giving the orders here,' he said, bringing the gun into view for the first time. 'Get the key.'

Sister Poole became more wary. Jez grabbed Bella and putting the barrel of the gun against her temple, he laughed wildly. Bella began to tremble.

'For the last time, get me that key.'

'Very well,' said Sister Poole. 'Release her first.'

'GET IT!' he howled.

The ward sister nodded and went into her office. But instead of getting the key to the Pharmacy, she picked up the telephone and pressed a button.

'We need help urgently in Regan Ward. There's a young man up here, demanding the key to the pharmacy. He's armed and dangerous. I can't stall him much longer. Please send—'

The receiver was snatched from her hand by Jez. Realising what the ward sister was doing, he pushed Bella into the office and interrupted the emergency call. With a burst of violence, he tore the telephone from its socket and threw it to the floor and stamped on it. Then he put his arm on the top of the desk and swept the contents wildly to the floor.

Alerted by the noise, a couple of nurses appeared, running. They backed off when he waved the gun at them. Sister Poole signalled to them to fetch help. Jez was becoming more and more angry now. He rounded on Sister Poole, waving the gun in the air.

'Why didn't you do as I told you?'

'I was only following the rules, Mr Halliday.'

'Rules! What rules! I make the rules around here.'

A uniformed security guard came sprinting down the corridor and peered in through the window. Soon, two male nurses joined him. They saw the situation at a glance and walked slowly towards the door.

'Get back!' roared Jez, grabbing Bella again.

'Now don't be difficult, sir,' said the security guard.

'Let her go,' said one of the male nurses.

The three men advanced but Jez soon put them to flight. Before they could get hold of him, he fired the gun at the ceiling and brought down a small avalanche of plaster. He'd made his point. The gun was loaded. The three men instantly froze in their tracks.

Jez put the barrel of the gun against Bella's head once again. She was trembling uncontrollably. The cold steel seemed to bore into her temple. Bella closed her eyes and prayed.

'Get out!' said Jez.

'Put that gun down,' advised the security guard.

'Then we can talk this over quietly,' added one of the male nurses. 'Tell us what you want and we'll see how we can help you. But we can't do that while you're holding that gun. Put it on the desk or someone may be hurt.'

'Out!' repeated Jez. 'Or she gets it!'

Two more security guards had arrived now and were looking in through the window. They watched as their colleague slowly backed out of the office with the two male nurses. Jez Halliday held the advantage for the moment and there was little they could do. Sister Poole and Bella were hostages.

Jez brought the gun round to point it at Bella's forehead. He was almost hysterical with excitement now.

'Stay back,' he yelled. 'Or I blow her brains out.'

CHAPTER SEVENTEEN

Jez Halliday was exhilarated. He enjoyed the sense of power the gun gave him. When the security guard and the male nurses left the room, he kicked the door shut. Then he pushed Bella down on to a chair and made Sister Poole sit down beside her. Several faces were now at the window. Jez stood behind the two women and moved the point of the gun from one to the other.

Bella was on the verge of collapse but Sister Poole remained icily calm. She put a reassuring hand on Bella's arm. It was also a signal to sit tight and do nothing.

Jez raised the gun and pointed it at the window.

'Get lost!' he yelled. 'I don't want to see your faces!'

The security guards and male nurses vanished at once.

Jez grinned. 'That's better.'

He was breathing heavily and his eyes blazed.

'You don't need the gun now,' said Sister Poole.

'Shut your face!'

'We'll do as you say. Put the gun down.'

Jez used the end of the barrel to flick off her cap.

'Where's that key?' he hissed.

'Mr Halliday...'

'Where is it?'

Now the gun was pressed against the back of her head. Sister Poole took a deep breath before speaking.

'It's in the top right-hand drawer of the desk,' she said. 'But that's locked as well. I have the key.'

'Hand it over.'

She took a bunch of keys nervously from her pocket.

'It's the smallest one,' she said, handing them over.

'It'd better be!'

Sister Poole relaxed as the gun was removed from her head. Bella looked sympathetically at her. She knew the horror of having the weapon nestling against her skull.

Jez was beginning to panic. He inserted the key and opened the drawer. Inside was a tray of keys with number tags attached to them.

'Which one is it?' he barked.

'Number seven,' replied Sister Poole.

He pulled out the tray, found the correct key then tossed the others to the floor. Bella and Sister Poole had their backs to him but they could see his reflection in the window. He looked more crazed than ever. Jez shouted at them.

'Let's go and open that door!' he said.

'You don't need us any more,' reasoned Sister Poole. 'You've got the key. Take what you want.'

'We won't stop you,' said Bella. 'We won't move.'

Jez lowered the gun as he thought it over. He swayed slightly then quickly regained his balance. He looked at the window but there was no sign of anyone. The pharmacy was only a few steps away. Jez thrust the gun back into his belt.

Bella and Sister Poole breathed a sigh of relief. They felt marginally safer. They were no longer being held at gunpoint. But their relief was short-lived. As Jez cautiously opened the door, a voice boomed out through a portable megaphone.

'This is the police! We are armed. Put down your weapon and come out now. Put down your weapon.'

Jez went mad. Slamming the door shut, he pulled out his gun and leapt at his two hostages. Bella felt the cold steel against her temple once more.

'Come and get me!' shouted Jez. 'I'm ready for you!'

Mark was propped up on pillows in his bed.

'How are you feeling now?' asked Suzie.

'A million times better,' he said.

'We'll look after you, Mark.'

'Yes,' said Gordy. 'You're in the right place. Bel can nurse you, Suze can take an X-ray and Kar can get you back on your feet with physio treatment.'

'What about you?' said Mark.

'I'm the doctor. My role is purely supervisory.'

'Then supervise us both a cup of coffee,' said

Suzie.

'I'll put the kettle on,' he agreed. 'But that's all. I have to get back to the hospital.' They heard the front door open. 'Is that you, Kar?' he called.

'Yes!' she called back. 'Where are you!'

'We're all in Mark's room!'

Karlene came charging up the stairs. She didn't even stop to ask what Mark was doing in bed.

'There's an emergency at the hospital!' she said.

'Nothing new in that,' observed Suzie.

'There's a man with a gun. He's taken hostages in East Wing. He's demanding drugs.

Gordy was alarmed. 'Did you say East Wing?'

'Yes,' said Karlene. 'One of the hostages is Bella!'

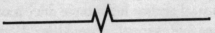

Bella was more terrified than ever. The arrival of armed police had roused Jez to a fever pitch of excitement. He was waving the gun about wildly and shouting obscenities. Anything could happen now. Bella feared she might not leave the office alive.

The voice was heard on the loud-hailer again.

'*Put your weapon down and come out now.*'

'Think I'm stupid!' yelled Jez.

'*The whole floor has been sealed off.*'

'That's what you think.'

'*Give yourself up now and nobody will get hurt.*'

'No way!' yelled Jez.

Male nurses could deal with most situations

inside the psychiatric unit but they weren't armed. As soon as they realised that Jez had a weapon, they had called the police. An armed response unit was at the hospital within minutes. Reinforcements were now arriving.

'*Come on out while you can!*' instructed the voice.

'Shove off.'

'*There's no way you can escape. Give yourself up now.*'

Jez's reply was dramatic. Aiming at the window, he pulled the trigger. The bullet shattered the glass and sent the pieces flying everywhere. Bella and Sister Poole instinctively covered their heads with their arms. Bella felt a trickle of blood on her face. She closed her eyes and prayed they'd get out alive.

'Did you hear that!' howled Jez. 'Back off!'

There was a long pause as the police considered the options. They brought one of the hospital's senior psychiatrists over to help. He'd been in hostage-situations before but never on his own doorstep.

He didn't use the loud-hailer. His voice could be heard quite clearly through the gaping window. His tone was soothing.

'This is Doctor Wilkes,' he said. 'I'm on my own. Can I come and talk to you?'

'No,' said Jez. 'Stay away.'

'I work here at the hospital. I may be able to

help.'

'It's a trick.'

'It's not, I promise you,' said the doctor. 'Is everyone all right in there?'

'At the moment!'

'I need some confirmation of that. Sister Poole?'

'We're not hurt, Doctor Wilkes.'

'And your companion?'

'We're all right,' confirmed Bella, nervously.

'They won't be for long!' warned Jez. 'Unless I get exactly what I want.'

'And what's that?'

'First of all, make the Bill back off.'

'They already have.'

'How do I know that?'

'Because you have my word for it,' the doctor reassured him. 'If you don't believe me, come out and see.'

'You're only trying to trap me.'

'I'm not armed. This corridor's empty.'

Jez needed a few moments to think about his next move. He had the key to the pharmacy in one hand and the gun in the other. Gesturing with the weapon, he made Bella get up from her chair and go to the door. She would be his shield. As she came out into the corridor, he was tucked in behind her. Bella was shaking uncontrollably.

The corridor was empty in both directions. A tall figure stepped cautiously into view. Doctor

Wilkes was a bald-headed man in a white coat. He held his arms out from his body to show he wasn't carrying a weapon.

'There's nobody else here,' he said, moving forward.

'Stay there!' snapped Jez.

The doctor halted. 'But we need to talk.'

'I can hear you.'

Doctor Wilkes could see how terrified Bella was.

'Let the young woman go,' he said. 'You don't need her any more. Or Sister Poole. Let them both go.'

'No!'

He took another step forward but the gun was pointed straight at him. Doctor Wilkes stopped again and shrugged. Bella was impressed. Even facing a deranged man with a gun, the doctor seemed calm.

'What do you want?' he asked.

'Something from in there,' said Jez, flicking the gun towards the pharmacy. 'I need supplies.'

'Do you have the key?'

'Yes.'

'Then what's stopping you? Take what you like. We have everything you want. Help yourself.'

'What about the police?'

'They're not here. It's just us. Go ahead.'

Jez suspected a trap. He looked up and down the corridor again but nobody else was in sight. The doors to the ward itself were shut tight.

'Would you like me to open the pharmacy for you?' said the doctor. 'I know where everything is.'

'I can do it myself.'

'Then why don't you?'

Jez hesitated. The doctor's manner had calmed him slightly. He made a plan. He'd help himself to all the drugs he needed then use Bella as a shield to get him safely out of the hospital. As long as he had her, they wouldn't dare touch him.

'Stay right where you are,' he ordered.

'Of course,' said the doctor. 'I won't move.'

'If I so much as see the Bill, she gets it.'

Bella gulped as she was pushed roughly towards the pharmacy. There seemed to be no escape for her. Jez was determined to hang on to his hostage.

Everything went very quiet. Bella could hear the fierce beating of her own heart. She stood in front of the door of the pharmacy while Jez fiddled with the key. He seemed less agitated now. Dr Wilkes had a calming effect on him.

In a flash, the situation changed. Voices were heard inside the ward — then a figure came bursting through the swing doors. It was Adam Green.

Jez stood behind Bella and pointed the gun at Adam.

'Let go of her, Jez!' said Adam.

'No!'

'Only cowards hide behind girls.'

'I'm not afraid of anything.'

'Adam,' said Doctor Wilkes, 'please go back into the ward. We can cope out here.'

'He's not going anywhere,' said Jez. 'He owes me.'

'Not any more.'

'Get it for me!' He pulled open the pharmacy door. 'You know what I want, Adam. Get it for me in there.'

'No, Jez. I'm out of that now.'

Bella was amazed by his courage. Adam was only six feet from the end of a loaded gun but he didn't look afraid.

'Move aside, Bella,' he said.

'I can't, he won't let me.'

'Step aside. This is between him and me.'

Adam's eyes were fixed on Jez. They were staring each other out. Bella moved very gently and found no resistance. She backed slowly down the corridor until she reached Doctor Wilkes. He gave her a comforting hug then pushed her behind him so his body was shielding her. Bella ran to safety.

Adam was still gazing into Jez's eyes.

'How did I get mixed up with scum like you?' he said.

'Don't push me, Adam.'

'I must have been mad.'

'Get me the drugs while you still can.'

'Get them yourself,' sneered Adam. 'That's your

world. Not mine. I've washed my hands of it. You helped kill Sarah. You were the one who got her on to cocaine. You're a murderer.'

Jez levelled the gun. 'Do as I tell you!'

Their eyes locked. Adam walked towards him.

'You haven't got the guts to pull that trigger.'

'Try me,' he spat.

'You're yellow, Jez. That's why everyone hates you.'

'Sarah didn't.' He grinned. 'She got to like me a lot.'

At that Adam lost all control. Sarah's name set him off and he launched himself at Jez, hitting him backwards against the wall. The gun went flying from Jez's hand. The two of them fell to the floor, fighting. Jez was strong but Adam was in a frenzy as he pinned him to the ground and punched him repeatedly. Blood began to pour down Jez's face.

Armed police ran out through the ward doors and overpowered both of them. Other policemen came from both ends of the corridor. Adam was pulled away before he could inflict any more wounds on his enemy. Jez was handcuffed and hauled off.

He was still yelling as they took him down in the lift.

Bella watched the struggle from a safe distance. She was full of admiration for Adam; he hadn't thought of his own safety for a moment. He'd needed to avenge Sarah.

Now the crisis was over, Bella was overcome with relief. She almost collapsed; her legs had turned to jelly. She'd been so close to death. It was an experience she never wanted to go through again. A nurse came to help her.

'Come and sit down. Can I get you anything?' she enquired. 'A cup of strong, sweet tea?'

'No, thanks,' said Bella. 'I just want to go home.'

— ⋀ — **EPILOGUE** — ⋀ —

Mark was reading in bed when there was a tap on his bedroom door. Louise came in with a large bunch of grapes. He was very surprised.

'Louise!' he gasped in delight.

'How are you, Mark?'

'All the better for seeing you.'

'I felt dreadful when they told me what had happened,' she said, coming over to him. 'Collapsing like that. I know how awful labyrinthitis can be. My father had it once.'

'It's not pleasant,' he admitted.

'Why didn't you tell me you felt so ill?'

'I didn't want you to think I was a wimp.'

'I'd never do that, Mark.' She kissed him on the cheek then handed over the grapes. 'I've brought these for you.'

'Thanks, Louise.'

It was the day after his collapse and he was feeling much better. Her unexpected visit was the best thing he could have wished for. He grinned at her. Louise was very apologetic.

'I'm really sorry for the way I behaved,' she said. 'I blamed you for being clumsy when you were ill. That's why you tipped that beer over me and knocked those books out of my hands.'

'I kept having dizzy spells,' he admitted.

'Why didn't you explain?'

'You didn't really give me the chance, Louise.'

'Well, I will next time,' she promised. 'And I've got some news that will cheer you up. Remember my silk shirt?'

'You've found a way to clean it?'

'No,' she said. 'That one is ruined. But it can be replaced free of charge.' She laughed at his astonishment. 'Isn't it fantastic? I nerved myself to tell my parents and they were very sweet. Turns out that Dad bought the shirt with his charge card. There's automatic insurance for any damage incurred within six weeks of buying anything.'

'That's great!'

'So you can stop feeling guilty. I'll wear the new shirt next time we go out together.' She lowered her eyes. 'If you still want to go out with me, that is.'

He took her hand and squeezed it between his palms.

'You bet!' he said. 'Does that mean I can buy those tickets for the dance?'

'No, Mark.' His face fell. She opened her bag and took out an envelope. 'Because I've already bought them. It's my way of saying sorry for being so mean to you.'

Mark felt over the moon. Her visit made him feel so much better he felt able to get out of bed after she'd gone. Karlene was on the telephone, Bella was stretched out on the sofa, her bare arms covered in sticking plaster where she'd been cut by flying glass at the hospital. Gordy was singing to himself in the kitchen.

'Mark!' said Bella. 'Shouldn't you be in bed.'

'Louise revived me,' he smiled.

'We won't ask how!'

He lowered himself carefully into a chair.

'How are you now, Bella?' he asked.

'Slowly getting over the shock. I'd hate to go through that experience again. It was terrifying.'

'Jez obviously needs psychiatric care.'

'Yes,' she said. 'It certainly helped Adam. He was the real hero. Even his stepmother was impressed. He rang me earlier to say they're letting him out of hospital soon.'

'That's encouraging.'

'He's hoping to turn over a new leaf.'

'What are the chances?'

'Who knows?' she said. 'But I gave him one piece of advice.'

'What was that?'

'He'd stolen a pendant from his stepmother, a wedding present. It really upset her. I told Adam she'd be eternally grateful if he could get it back somehow.'

'Do you think he can?' asked Mark.

'Easily. It's hidden in his room. Adam didn't steal it to sell for money. He just wanted to spite her. When she gets that pendant back, she'll be thrilled. Anyway, that's my last connection with the Green family. I went in too deep and I paid the penalty. I've signed off now. They can sort out their own problems.'

Karlene put down the receiver and joined them.

'Look at you two,' she said. 'Pair of old crocks.'

'We've only had one day off,' said Bella.

Karlene grinned. 'You deserve it, Bella. They ought to give you a medal for what you went through.'

'Rather not talk about it, if you don't mind.'

'Who was on the phone?' said Mark.

'Mrs Tyc. I never thought she'd ring but she did. She's got a violent husband. I told her she didn't have to go on putting up with him. I gave her a contact number to put her in touch with a social worker. She didn't realise there was so much help available. The social worker has been a big help already. She just rang to thank me.'

'Well done!' said Mark.

'All I did was show an interest in her.'

'That's more than anyone else did, Karlene.'

Gordy came in from the kitchen with a big grin on his face.

'Doctor Robbins is just making his ward rounds,' he said. 'What can I get the patients?'

'A plate of pasta covered in Dolmio sauce,' said Bella.

'Not for me,' added Mark.

'What about something hot to warm you up?'

'She's just been,' said Bella. 'Louise Webb.'

They were all laughing as Suzie let herself into the house. She was the last home from the hospital that evening and seemed in good spirits. She said hello to her friends and asked after the patients.

'I feel terrific,' said Mark.

'I'm getting there,' said Bella, warily.

'Well, I've just heard some great news about another patient,' said Suzie. 'Remember I mentioned that little girl? Donna French? They've finally found one.'

'A white rabbit?'

'No, idiot! A donor!'

'Who wants to donate a white rabbit?'

'A *kidney* donor!' said Suzie. 'They may be able to perform a transplant operation, after all. I feel so happy for her. Donna deserves a bit of good luck.'

'So do we all!' said Gordy.

'I've had mine,' said Mark. 'Louise's visit.'

'Mrs Tyc was mine,' added Karlene. 'Bella?'

'After yesterday, I feel lucky just to be alive,' she said.

'That only leaves you, Gordy,' said Suzie. 'What would really cheer you up?'

'Easy answer to that, Suze,' he said with a sly grin. 'How would you fancy coming to *Underworld* with me? It's a riot!'

Laughing, the four of them groaned and hurled cushions at him.

Lions

CITY HOSPITAL
SERIES
by Keith Miles

Discover City Hospital and the five young
recruits who work there. Experience the high
drama and the humour of life in a large, modern
hospital. Everything from romance to
radiotherapy - drama to drudgery, from fun to
fatigue. If you can take the pressure, it's all here!

CITY
HOSPITAL

NEW BLOOD

As soon as the ambulance stopped, its doors opened and the stretcher was lifted swiftly but gently to the ground. The small boy with the chubby face lay pale and motionless on his back. As one of the paramedics wheeled him into Casualty, another walked alongside, holding the plastic bottle that was attached to his arm by a tube.

Dr Damian Holt was waiting with a nurse in a bay that was curtained off by a plastic sheet. One look at the patient told him that the boy was in a critical condition.

Two lives hang in the balance at City Hospital - but Suzie's involvement in the first means her life is in danger too.

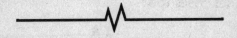

CITY HOSPITAL

FLAMES

Karlene retched as the smoke got into her throat. Coughing himself, Mark led her away from the blaze. For a few minutes, they could do nothing but wait and watch. After what seemed like a lifetime to the waiting crowd, the inferno seemed finally under control. There was a loud hissing noise and two firemen with breathing apparatus were checking to see if it was safe to go into the building.

A new sound cut through the pandemonium. It was the high-pitched scream of a girl, who was racing along the street towards them.

'No!' she shrieked. 'Not our house!'

Emotional trauma is part of daily life in City Hospital - but can the new recruits cope with personal crises too?

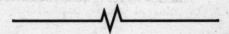

CITY HOSPITAL

FEVER

Bella was stunned. 'Mrs Elliott isn't dead is she?'

'Yes, I'm afraid so. We did all we could but...' Her voice trailed off - she looked shocked and confused herself.

'What was the cause of death?'

Sister Morgan's face changed. Bella had never seen her look like that before; a look of fear and bewilderment. It was as if she'd come up against something completely outside her experience. It scared her. She bit her lip and shook her head sadly.

'We don't know, Bella,' she admitted. 'We just don't know.'

Will someone crack under the strain, as feelings run to fever-pitch at City Hospital?

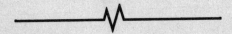